TOP 40 HONEYPOT

CALUMET EDITIONS

Minneapolis

10 9 8 7 6 5 4 3 2 1

ISBN: 978-1-962834-14-8

Cover and book design by Gary Lindberg

TOP 40 HONEYPOT

JANET MERRAN

**CALUMET
EDITIONS**
Minneapolis

Part One

1

Tuesday, July 9, 1974
Billboard Hot 100 Hit Song of the Week:
"Rock the Boat" by The Hues Corporation

My love of radio started when I was a kid. I was born in a small town in northern Iowa—population 1,729, whose most notable native son was a wrestling coach in the Iowa Sports Hall of Fame. My dad worked for the post office and my mom worked in the school cafeteria, two ordinary parents who never missed church on Sunday, 4th of July fireworks, Harvest fest, or Santa's parade. It was a bucolic and simple life.

Growing up, we didn't have a television, so every evening after supper, my parents huddled around the radio, listening to their favorites. Mom liked comedies, *Ozzie and Harriet* or *Jack Benny*, and Dad liked CBS *Radio Mystery Theater*. They grew up in the heyday of radio dramas, but I liked something different—Top 40 radio.

My grandparents got me my own radio for my twelfth birthday in 1961. I'd stay up late at night listening while I did my homework. It was just before the British Invasion, when the Beatles came to America and changed music forever. My favorites were Elvis Presley, Patsy Cline, Roy Orbison and Chubby Checker. As my voice got lower, I dreamed of becoming a boss jock at a Top 40 radio station.

3

In high school, I started hanging around the local station, doing odd jobs, and just like in the movies, I got a chance to go on the radio one day when a guy didn't show up for work. By graduation, my career path was clear. I was hired as a weekend disc jockey at that small-town station. I taught myself audio production and how to make an aircheck audition tape. I moved up, traveling across the country, one radio station at a time, for seven years, until I became a DJ at a highly rated Top 40 station in Houston in the Harkins Media radio chain.

That's where I met Vince Johnson, the program director. Vince taught me everything about the business, including all the tricks of top-notch production. He became my best friend. It was always obvious that Vince was headed for an executive-level position. He used his connections and moved on very quickly. Now Vince is the national program director for Harkins Media.

Top 40 had changed a lot since it started in the 1950s, and Henry Harkins was a huge contributor to that change. Now Top 40 radio had precise planning. Each song, each jingle, and the patter of the disc jockeys was all calculated. It was a real science, done with planning and research, and Harkins Media was leading the way.

People no longer sat in their homes listening to radio dramas. Television had taken over as home entertainment. Radio had to change with the times. Now you could listen as you went about your daily business, in the car, or anywhere you could bring a portable radio.

Henry Harkins was part of a large, well-educated family that had been in the radio business since the late 1940s. He started in his home state of Michigan, buying, upgrading, and then selling stations—making a lot of money along the way. It didn't hurt that he had unseen investors from the Organization, who made sure no one interfered with Henry Harkins.

By the time I got involved, Harkins Media owned five stations in Michigan, Texas, Nevada, Kansas, and California. When Harkins acquired a station, he would send in his own team. He had his own people; engineers, accountants, and consultants, review the books and inspect the studios. The engineers would upgrade the broadcast equipment and increase the power or change the tower site. The new general manager would hire his own sales team and staff; and the new program director would hire his own music director and jocks, change the programming, get the ratings up, and overwhelm the market with big-money contests. The competition never knew what hit them.

When Harkins entered a market, he responded to the needs of the community. The Top 40 stations had a special mix of music, news, DJ chatter, public service announcements, and commercials. The songs were picked from five categories: the weekly top hits, a song that had just fallen off the charts, a song with broad appeal, a song gaining momentum, and a new release. They also used slick pre-recorded jingles for station identification.

The disc jockeys used sound effects with echo chambers, sound filters, and other technological gizmos to create signature sounds for fun and excitement. When you threw in the contests, promotions, and cash giveaways, it was hard *not* to listen to a Harkins station.

Beach City Top 40 in California was one of the most popular stations in the country. Originally, the station had been a major network affiliate, but when Henry Harkins bought it in the 1960s, he changed the format to Top 40 . He also moved the station from downtown Beach City to an undeveloped area in a new building next to the 50,000-watt transmitter tower.

The station was always popular, but it really hit the big time in the early 1970s with an extravagant contest run by a brilliant program director named Ben Bailey. Later, Bailey ran a company that provided innovative research to maximize Arbitron ratings for his client stations. He even used computers, which was extremely ahead of the times.

Vince and I kept in close touch with Ben Bailey after he started his business. I sent him airchecks and samples of my production work and made him promise to eventually get me an interview to be a program director for one of the Harkins stations.

That was how I found myself, at the age of twenty-five, on my way to New York City to be interviewed for the best job I could ever imagine. I, Donnie Dixon, the small-town kid who loved radio, was applying for the job of program director at Beach City Top 40, the jewel of the Harkins chain.

On a bright, hot morning in July, Vince met me at LaGuardia. I immediately recognized him with his long brown ponytail, Eagles t-shirt, jeans, and high-top Chuck Taylors.

"Vince, good to see you man," I said.

"Donnie, dude, lookin' good."

I put down my backpack and pumped his hand, smiling.

"Grab your stuff and we'll get a taxi to Midtown. Everyone is anxious to meet you."

"I'm ready; let's go."

I followed my friend outside to the taxi stand, where we got a cab to the Manhattan headquarters of Harkins Media. After that plane ride I needed a smoke, so I lit up a cig.

Forty minutes later, as we stood in front of a bank of elevators, Vince said, "We're on the fifteenth floor. Follow me into my office and I'll give you a rundown on who you're gonna meet. Chew some gum for a minute to freshen your breath. And you can comb your hair, too."

Once we were in his suite, I put down my backpack, found my comb, and ran it through my hair. He threw a stick of gum at me. I chewed it for a minute, then spat it back into the wrapper and threw it in the trash.

"How's my breath? Am I dressed okay for this meeting?" I was wearing jeans, sneakers, and a Rolling Stones t-shirt.

"You're fine. This is radio. You aren't expected to be a fashion plate—you're expected to pull in ratings."

I sat on a chair across from Vince's desk. I looked around at the modern décor and the view of the Manhattan skyline. "Man, this is a great office. Who'll be at the meeting?"

"There'll be three people: Nick Mitchell, Elizabeth Corley, and Henry Harkins. Henry says he's met you before."

"Yeah, once, but I never really talked to him. I was just a DJ. We were introduced when he visited the station in Houston. He seemed to like me."

"That's good. The other two are Nick and Elizabeth. They came here from the Michigan station. Nick Mitchell's an old-school guy who's been in radio since the 1950s. He became a program director in the sixties for Harkins. Now he's the executive vice-president of the chain. He demands complete loyalty. I've heard stories about him."

"Like what?"

"Like, if one of his jocks got in a financial jam, he'd peel off a couple hundred bucks from a roll of fifties without asking questions. But if you piss him off, you'll get kicked out the door so fast it will take five seconds for your ass to catch up. But he respects what we do and he's always got our back— as long as you remember that it's always about the bottom line."

I nodded. "Got it."

"Elizabeth Corley, now she's the one to watch out for. She's the national music director. She'll be wearing a black suit. She started out as Nick's secretary, but now she's the go-to girl for just about everything. She's a stunner, but with her it's all business. Be careful what you tell her—it'll go straight to Nick."

"I'll remember that."

"Henry Harkins is proud of how he's built the business from nothing. He's got friends in high places, friends you don't ask about. At this point, he really likes you, especially after all the great stuff I told him."

"Anything else I should know?"

"They already want to hire you, so don't blow it. Just be polite and go along with whatever they say. Come on; let's go. We don't want to keep them waiting."

I followed Vince into the board room. It had a large, polished table and a wall of windows that looked out onto the city. The three executives were waiting for me. Harkins looked intimidating in his custom three-piece suit. I tried not to be nervous when Vince led me to my seat across from Harkins.

Vince introduced me. "Henry, Nick, Elizabeth, this is Donald Dixon."

Henry Harkins stood up and extended his hand.

I shook it and said, "How do you do, sir? I'm happy to meet you."

"Welcome, Donald. What do you think of New York?"

"It's very impressive, sir."

"You don't have to call me sir, just Henry." Then he turned toward his executives. "This is Nick Mitchell, our executive vice-president, and Elizabeth Corley, our national music director."

"It's very nice to meet both of you." They got up and I shook their hands in turn. Elizabeth was very ladylike; she barely touched my hand.

I turned back to Henry. "You can call me Donnie; it's my radio name."

"Okay, then, Donnie. You come very highly recommended. So, tell us why you want to be the program director at Beach City Top 40."

I pulled my chair in close, sat up straight, and started my pitch.

"As you know, I've been working in radio ever since I was in high school. Top 40 is in my blood. I've worked my way up at five stations in the past seven years. Now I'm at your Houston station, where I met Vince."

"Vince speaks highly of you, Donnie," Nick said. "We've been watching your ratings and listening to your airchecks. Very impressive."

"Thank you, Mr. Mitchell."

"You can call me Nick."

"Thank you, Nick. I'm really good at production, and I love to run contests. One of my heroes is Ben Bailey, who was at Beach City Top 40 for years."

"He's a consultant for us now," Henry said.

"Yes, I've heard. I'd like to follow in his footsteps."

"What about music, Donnie?" asked Elizabeth.

"I'll use the Harkins method, of course, and I'd like to use Ben Bailey's research to tighten up the playlists for maximum retention of listeners."

"Good answer, Donnie," she said. "Do have any problem with taking direction from New York on your weekly music adds?"

"Not at all, Elizabeth. I'll be able to hire a music director, won't I?"

"Yes. We like our program directors to have assistance."

I looked at Nick and asked, "Will I have a good budget for promotions and contests?"

Nick nodded. "Beach City Top 40 is the jewel of our chain. You'll have enough cash and prizes to keep us on top. You'll work directly with the station general manager on budget."

"That sounds great," I said.

"Do you have any other questions?" Henry asked.

"None that I can think of." I figured it'd be wisest not to ask anything. I didn't want to risk sounding stupid.

Henry said, "Then I'd like to offer you the job of program director at Beach City Top 40, Donnie. How soon can you start?"

I was stunned. I thought I'd have to jump through hoops and navigate multiple interviews.

"I can start in a couple of weeks, but I'll need a good salary and a stipend for moving." I paused and decided to shoot for the moon. "I need thirty thousand to start, and a grand to move."

"I think we can do that," Harkins said, nodding. "And there will be bonuses if you help us with special projects. Are we agreed?"

"Agreed," I said.

It was that easy and that quick.

Soon the meeting was over. I followed Vince into his office, and he shut the door. I sighed with relief. "Wow. That went well."

"Yeah Donnie, you're getting the break of a lifetime. I hope you appreciate it."

"Believe me, I do."

"And you're going to be swamped with work. Are you ready for it?"

A twinge of fear and doubt ran through me. I stuffed it back down and simply said, "I am."

2

Monday, August 5, 1974
Billboard Hot 100 Hit Song of the Week:
"Annie's Song" by John Denver

A s soon as I got back from New York, I started planning
for my big move. I was newly married to Carol, a divorcée
with a six-year-old son. Carol and I had met through Vince.
She was a sister of one of his radio buddies. After a whirl-
wind courtship, I asked her to be mine, and we went down to
City Hall and made it official.

Now I had a new job, and a new wife, and Jason, my new
stepson. I was the luckiest guy in the world except that Carol
couldn't move out to join me in California until she sold her
house.

I didn't have any problem giving notice at the Houston station. In radio there's always someone ready to take your place.

My first day at the new job was scheduled for Monday,
August 5, so in the last week in July, I packed a suitcase and
headed west in my new yellow Camaro. The station set me
up in a nice hotel in the city, and I spent my first weekend
getting acquainted with the area.

I quickly found a rental duplex by the beach. I met the
landlord, wrote a check for the first and last month's rent,

and the place was mine. Then I went back to my hotel to call Carol and Vince.

The first time I drove out to Beach City Top 40, I almost got lost because it was so far out in the country. But when I saw the six-element directional array against the scrub, I knew I was in the right place. The building was an unassuming brown ranch-style office with a parking lot on the side. Another small building, just beyond the lot, housed the broadcasting equipment.

I spent the rest of the weekend driving around the city, listening to Beach City Top 40, and making mental notes of the things I liked about the programming and the things I wanted to change.

Vince gave me the lowdown on the station's general manager, Earl Fredrickson. Earl was in his forties, a big dude who had played football in college. He started his radio career right after graduation, not as a DJ, but in sales. His second job was as the general manager of an FM station in Indiana. In the early 1970s, Earl moved to a Michigan station with a Top 40 format, which also happened to compete with a station owned by Henry Harkins. He did such a good job that Harkins decided to crush the competition by hiring Earl away. He had been at Beach City for about two years.

On Monday I got to the station promptly at 9:00, parked my Camaro, walked in the front door, and asked for Mr. Fredrickson. A tall, curvy secretary with a blonde bouffant took me into Earl's office. Earl got up from his desk and grabbed my hand.

"Hello, Donnie, welcome to Beach City!" He had close-cropped salt-and-pepper hair, black rimmed glasses, and wore a custom-tailored tropical wool suit. His enthusiastic handshake almost crushed my hand.

"Pleased to meet you, Mr. Fredrickson."

"Call me Earl."

"Okay, Earl."

He turned to his secretary. "Jenny, this is Donnie Dixon, our new program director."

"Hello, Donnie," she said, holding out her hand.

"Hi, Jenny."

"That will be all, Jenny. Could you close the door as you leave?"

I watched her as she left the room. Her high heels showed off a great ass, though she was a little old for my taste.

Earl peered down at me. "How are you liking our fair city so far? Is your hotel room comfortable?"

"Everything is great. I already rented a place by the beach, and I spent the weekend listening to the station and taking notes. I can't wait to get started."

"We've been a ship without a captain for two weeks since our last program director left. I hope you're ready to dig in and work."

"I certainly am," I said.

"That's terrific. How about we start with a tour of the station? After you get your bearings, you can start tackling the pile on your desk. Tomorrow, I have some production work I need done, but we'll talk about that later."

"Solid."

We stepped out of his office for a tour of the building. In the front were the fancy offices, for him and the sales team. They would be gathering in an hour for their weekly Monday morning meeting. As we walked by, Earl stopped to introduce me to a young lady sitting at her desk. Later he told me she was the first salesgirl the station had ever hired.

"Karen, you're here early. Good. I like a go-getter. Do you have a minute?"

13

She put down her pen and looked up from her appointment book. "Good morning, Earl. I always have time for you."

"Karen, this is Donnie Dixon, our new program director. Today is his first day."

She stood up and extended her hand with a big smile. "Nice to meet you, Donnie. Welcome to Beach City Top 40."

"Same here." Karen was a looker. She had long legs, shiny brown hair, and a short mini skirt. I bet she didn't have any problem closing deals.

"I've got to prep for the week now," she said, "but I hope we can work on a promotion together sometime."

"I hope so, too."

Earl pointed over my shoulder. "You can meet the other salesmen later. Let me take you over to the staff areas."

We walked to a spacious room in the middle of the building. It was filled with desks for the girls who did payroll and scheduled the advertising. Earl walked me over to two of them, one busy at her typewriter and the other chewing on the end of her pen, a stack of paperwork in front of her. They both looked up at the boss.

"Good morning, girls," Earl said.

"Good morning, Mr. Fredrickson," they answered in unison.

"Say hello to Donnie Dixon, our new program director."

"Hello," said the pen chewer, a busty brunette in a sleeveless shift. "I'm Michelle." She extended her hand.

"Nice to meet you."

"And this is Stephanie," Earl said. "She's indispensable."

"Sorry about the mess," she told me as she stood and offered her hand. "I'm up to my ears in work." She was a tall brown-haired girl in a skirt and tie-neck blouse. Vince had told me about her. She was the fiancée of one of the DJs, Rockin' Rex Rogers. She had worked at the station since high school.

"It's a pleasure to meet you," I said.

We continued down the corridor past the telephone switchboard, where a Hispanic chick in a short skirt with headsets and microphone was busy answering and connecting calls. She looked up for a moment and waved hello. Then we were in the long hall in the programming wing of the building.

One side of the hall had the restrooms and kitchen. The other side had two production studios, the newsroom, and offices that would be for me and my music director. At the very end of the hall was the control booth with the disc jockey. Tucked in the corner was a small room with a phone for the request lines, though no one was manning it. Like all radio stations, there were speakers playing the broadcast for everyone in the building to hear.

We stopped in front of the room that would be my office.

"This is your new home, Donnie. I hope you like it."

It was a big, comfortable room with a large desk, two extra chairs, a file cabinet and shelves, and a sofa pushed against the wall for late nights.

"I love it." I noticed a huge stack of mail, records, carts, packages, and other assorted radio stuff piled on the desk.

Earl eyed the pile and said, "I told you there was plenty to do. But first check out the newsroom. It's this way." He pointed down the hall.

We walked into the newsroom, where a small balding man in a short-sleeved white shirt and bow tie was holding the Associated Press ticker and scribbling notes. He quickly got up when he saw the boss.

"Norman, this is our new program director, Donnie Dixon. Donnie, this is Norman Morris, the best newsman in Beach City."

"Hi, Donnie, welcome to Beach City Top 40."

"Great to meet you, Norman." Vince had told me about Norman. He was a total straight arrow—dull but smart and dependable. "I'm told you've been with the station for 20 years."

"Yes. Things have changed a lot, but everyone always needs the news."

"Carry on," Earl told him.

It was an FCC regulation that our station broadcast news every hour. If it were up to me, I'd get rid of the news. No one listened to Beach City Top 40 for its news coverage. But because of the FCC, Norman had a job for life. We left him to write his stories for the next broadcast.

"Our morning man just got off his shift," Earl said. "I see him in the production studio. Let's go in and say hello."

Inside, I saw a jock with a bunch of scripts sitting in front of the mike. To my surprise, it was one of my former buddies, Matt West. Years ago, Matt and I had briefly worked together at a station in Denver. I had no idea that he was a DJ at Beach City Top 40.

"Hey, dude! How are you?" I asked.

"Donnie, buddy! I heard you were on your way. I didn't realize you'd be here today." He gave me a quick pat on the back. "Hey, I heard you got hitched!"

"You heard right. Carol and I have been married for all of two months."

"Congratulations, man! You're gonna love Beach City. It's a happenin' town."

"I can see. This is gonna be great, especially with you here, Matt."

Matt was a little older than the other jocks, slightly pudgy and balding, a fact he tried to conceal with a toupée. Matt was great at ad-libbing and zany morning show antics, but never made a mistake or lost his cool on air. He'd been in radio since the mid-1960s and was well respected in the field.

Matt scribbled some numbers on a piece of paper and handed it to me.

"Donnie, here's my number; give me a call tonight. We can grab dinner. Let's catch up."

"Sure thing, dude."

"Let's finish the tour," Earl said. "I want you to meet our mid-morning guy, Charlie Greene."

We shut the door of the production room and continued down the hall to the control booth. It was a typical broadcast setup, a small room with a big glass window. The jocks sat at a desk with the control panel, the microphone, and other equipment; behind them were wire racks for the music carts. The big red light outside the studio was on and the DJ was in the booth, talking.

When we got to the control booth. Earl and I watched for a few minutes while Charlie started his set. He was a long-haired, mustachioed guy wearing a tucked-in blue button-down pulled over his beer belly. When the microphone light went off, we both stepped inside the control booth.

"Charlie, this is Donnie Dixon, our new program director."

"Good to meet you, man," Charlie said, extending his hand.

"Nice to meet you, Charlie. Great set. I've looked at your numbers and you're really tearing up mid-mornings. Those housewives love you."

Like all Harkins stations, Beach City Top 40 altered its programming for different listeners at different times of the day. Mid-morning radio was the accompaniment for office workers and housewives. During those hours, the station played softer sounds and female vocalists.

Charlie smiled. "That's me—the housewives' mid-morning companion." Looking at the clock, and then us, he said, "Hang tight, I'm back on in three...two...one...."

We stood quietly, listening to Charlie's on-air patter, until he put on "Annie's Song," the number one hit of the week, and turned off the mike. We nodded goodbye, and me and Earl stepped outside the control room.

"Let's go back to my office, Donnie. There are a few more things I want to discuss."

We walked back through the station to his office. Earl shut the door and sat down behind his polished mahogany desk.

"Okay Donnie, what do you think?"

"I'm impressed. The place is great. I really like the production studio. You know, production is my specialty."

"I'm told you're a whiz in the studio—and a real team player."

"Yes I am, Earl." What else was I going to say?

"Today I'll work up your weekly production schedule of commercials and voice-adds. First thing tomorrow we can sit down again and talk about the contests we'll be doing between now and the end of the year. We're in the middle of a contest right now called Tie a Yellow Ribbon. I'll fill you in on the details later." He looked at the leather appointment book on his desk. "No, wait a minute. I have a breakfast meeting first thing tomorrow. How about 11:00?"

"That's fine. I'll make a list of things I've been thinking about."

"That's great. Do you have any questions for me?"

"I do. There's one thing I'd like to settle now if that's okay. Can I go ahead and hire Patrick Thomas for music director? We go back a long way in radio. He's the best there is."

"Is he really the best guy for the job?"

"Absolutely," I answered. "You're going to love him. I have his aircheck in my car if you want to hear it."

Earl shook his head. "I'll take your word for it. What kind of salary does he need?"

"Low 20s," I said, hoping the figure wasn't too high.

"If you can bring him on for 22 or less a year, he's your man."

Wow. Another slam dunk. "I'll call him today."

Earl looked at his Rolex. "Donnie, I'm having lunch with a new advertiser, and I have to get going. The jocks are all looking forward to meeting you. Later I'll fill you in on which are the smart ones, and which are clueless. Any questions?"

"Yeah," I said. "I noticed there wasn't anyone taking requests."

"You're right, Donnie. I'm glad you brought it up. Right now, we only take requests on weekends. Henry Harkins and I were just talking about the request lines the other day. He told me he wants us to add more hours for better research."

I nodded enthusiastically. "Great idea."

"I'll let you know when I get the okay to get it up and running." Earl stood up and straightened his suit jacket. "Okay, Donnie, Beach City Top 40 is yours now. I'm expecting the best from you."

His eyes met mine, and suddenly his demeanor became deeply serious. "Don't mess it up," he warned.

Then he pushed past me and disappeared down the hall.

3

Monday, August 16, 1974
Billboard Hot 100 Hit Song of the Week:
"Feel Like Makin' Love" by Roberta Flack

The contest was called Tie a Yellow Ribbon, and today we were going to pick the winner live at the Beach City mall. I had to drive over there with all the correct entries and make sure everything was set up properly for the remote. Earl had filled me in on the details of the contest and the way it was going down.

The contest was simple: the listeners had to count the number of times a particular song was played over a three-week period. At the end, they had three days to mail or hand deliver a postcard to the station with their number of guesses. If they had the right number, the card would be entered into a drawing for ten thousand dollars. I had a giant fishbowl full of entries that I'd wrapped with yellow ribbons.

We chose the number one hit from last year, "Tie a Yellow Ribbon 'Round the Ole Oak Tree" as the song. I was pushing the contest hard to lead into the fall ratings. I had the image of a yellow ribbon printed on the week's "Hit Sheet," and produced lots of jingles and promos. We played the song during all sorts of weird times, like halfway through the weather and traffic reports, to keep people listening as long as possible.

I wondered how many of our listeners knew what the song was about. A guy just out of prison is on the bus coming home after three years, and he has written his sweetheart to tie a yellow ribbon around the tree to signal if she still wants him. When he gets there, he sees that she tied a hundred ribbons around the tree to show her love, and everybody on the bus cheers for him. Who says romance is dead?

Our afternoon guy, Rockin' Rex Rogers, was going to pick the winner. Rex first arrived at Beach City in the early 1970s. Like me, he'd loved radio since he was a kid. He grew into a bear of a man who always wore his signature outfit of a cowboy hat, Western shirt, and boots. He was known for his high energy and fast patter. Whenever the station held an event, he always drew a crowd. He also donated lots of time and money to charity.

I got there early to supervise the tech guys setting up the remote, and I was pleased to see over three hundred people already gathered. I hid the fishbowl with all the entries under the table to pull out at the right time.

At about ten minutes before 2:00 p.m., I spied Rex and his fiancée Stephanie making their way through the crowd.

"Dude, we're here." Rex strode up, nodding at his fans along the way, and climbed the three steps to take his place on the stage. Stephanie stood to the side, I knew she and would melt back into the crowd as soon as Rex started his patter.

"Hey, Stephanie, lookin' good today," I said. She had on a cute striped dress that showed off her long legs.

"Thanks, Donnie," she said, blushing a bit.

The stage had been set up with a small table and all the equipment for the remote, including loudspeakers blasting our station for the crowd. Rex sat down in front of the microphone and got comfortable with his headsets. My guys had the feed set up, so the songs were played in our studio, but the DJ's microphone was live, and it transmitted without any delays. It would all be seamless to the listener. The mall had even set up decorations for us: bunches of yellow balloons tied with yellow ribbons, on both sides of the stage. A big station banner stretched across the front.

For the next three and a half hours, Rex slowly built the excitement of the contest. Around five-thirty he asked anyone who had sent in a postcard to come and stand in front. You didn't have to be there to win, but it was always more fun when the winner was present. As the afternoon wore on, more and more people had showed up.

I'd told Rex to announce that the contest drawing would be at 5:45 p.m., when we had a maximum number of listeners. As the time drew near, the anxious crowd pressed closer and closer to the front of the stage. I was standing on the side with a little cluster of station people, including my evening jock, James Ryan, as well as some of the station girls, who had come to the mall to watch the spectacle.

It was finally time to pick the winner. The number one song of last month, "Rock Your Baby" by George McCrae, was winding down. I walked up the stairs, took a seat next to Rex, and put on headsets to talk to him while he worked the crowd.

Rex switched on his microphone and greeted the audience. "Man, we're having such a good time. Seeing so many nice faces and meeting so many nice people and saying hello. Man, I'll tell you, this is definitely the place! Beach City Top 40!" The crowd roared in approval.

"You better believe it, we're gonna have a winner. Right now, I'm giving away, ten . . . thousand . . . dollars, right here, on Beach City Top 40!"

I leaned into the second mike. "How many entries do we have, Rex?"

"Hundreds, Donnie; take them out! Ladies and gentlemen, say hello to our Beach... City... Top... 40... program director... Donnie Dixon!"

The crowd roared, "Hello, Donnie!" I pulled out the fishbowl of postcards from under the table.

"Hey, Donnie, are we ready to pick a winner?"

"We sure are, Rockin' Rex. And you can do the honors."

"How many times did we play the song?" Rex yelled.

"We played it one hundred and seven times," I shot back.

"And how many correct entries did we get?" he said.

"Four hundred and twenty. And here they are!" I pushed the fishbowl right in front of him.

I'd given Rex his instructions the day before . He was to pick the postcard with two paper clips attached to the side, and surreptitiously push the clips off before he pulled out the card.

"Here we go, ladies and gentlemen, boys and girls."

Rockin' Rex shoved his hand into the batch of correct entries. It took him a long time to find the right one. He grinned at the crowd as if he were deliberately teasing them. The crowd shouted back at him: "Pick! Pick! Pick!"

I felt relieved as he pulled out the winning entry and announced, "Are you ready?" he yelled.

"Yeah!" roared the crowd.

"Are you sure you're ready?" Rex screamed, even louder.

"Yeah!" The crowd yelled back, even louder.

"Are you positive you're ready?" Rex worked the crowd as only he could.

"We're ready!" They roared in return.

Then, triumphantly holding up the postcard, Rex crowed at the top of his lungs. "We have a winner!" Looking closely at the postcard, he shouted, "Our winner is Jimmy Harvey from right here in Beach City! Are you here Jimmy?"

A young-looking surfer dude, in board shorts and a t-shirt, ran up to the stage, waving his arms in excitement. I didn't know the exact connection, but the kid was probably the son of a big advertiser.

"What's your favorite radio station?" Rex asked the excited kid, reaching over so they could both yell into the mike.

They both screamed, "Beach! City! Top! 40! Beach! City! Top 40!"

By then everyone else was jumping up and down on the stage, and the crowd in the front was clapping and cheering.

Rex sat back down and the winning song, "Tie a Yellow Ribbon," played over the loudspeakers, while the crowd settled down. I took off my headsets and talked to the kid, getting his contact information. I told him I'd be sending him all the forms to claim his prize. I also told him to send me a copy of his driver's license to verify that he was 18 or older.

Rex finished up his shift with his signature goodbye: "I'm Rockin' Rex Rogers, king of the dial, from Beach City Top 40. Keep on keepin' on and I'll be back soon!"

The guys at the remote switched everything back to the studio. The crowd dispersed, and Rex and Stephanie split. I finally had time to break for a cig.

By now it was twilight. The stars were just coming out, and the air was cooling down from the heat of the day. I looked around to enjoy the moment and thought about how far I'd come from my little hometown station.

As soon as I got back, I'd make a cart of Rockin' Rex and the winner screaming the station name in the peak of their excitement. We'd play it over and over for the next two days.

In a few more weeks, we'd be on to the next contest. I silently hoped not all our contests were dirty.

4

Tuesday, September 10, 1974
Billboard Hot 100 Hit Song of the Week:
"(You're) Having My Baby" by Paul Anka with Odia Coates

The week after Labor Day, I got a message that Earl Fredrickson wanted to see me in his office. I walked over to his side of the building, and Jenny showed me into his office and closed the door.

"Sit down, Donnie, sit down."

I wasn't nervous: I knew I'd been performing well. I had a great lineup of disc jockeys, and my good friend Patrick Thomas was doing the 6:00 to 10:00 p.m. slot. Patrick was as happy to be the music director as I was to have him. It was a bitchin' team.

"Tell me, Donnie, how are you liking everything so far?"

"This place is great! I'm only missing one thing—my new wife. She's still in Houston because she has to sell her house. Also, her kid just started first grade and she doesn't want to uproot him right now."

Earl nodded. "Listen, Donnie, you can call her anytime on the station phone, at our expense. So, tell me, are you pleased with the station lineup?"

"The guys are top notch."

I meant it, too. Our DJs were known and respected, both in radio and the community. With 50,000 watts, our station was heard up and down the coast for miles, and we were always at the top of the ratings.

Our morning man was Matt West; the midday man was Charlie Greene; the afternoon DJ was Rockin' Rex Rogers; Patrick Thomas did evenings; and the late evening man was James Ryan. We had an overnight guy, Keith Adams, and on weekends, Dean Young, and Sammy Talarico. I did weekend mornings so the regulars could have a day off, and fill-ins when one of the boys got sick or went on vacation.

Earl nodded. "Yes they are, Donnie. Now, our sales team just landed some new accounts and they need commercials. Also, I need you to check all the station jingles and sound effects carts; some might need to be redubbed. I don't want anything breaking on the air."

Our station had made a variety of five-second cartridges: professional vocalists singing the station name, funny sound effects, and special carts to introduce each DJ. These were perfect for the rapid sequences between songs during the air shifts. The songs we played were recorded on the carts too, because 45s could scratch, wear out, or break.

"I'll take care of it," I said.

I started to get up, but Earl motioned me to sit back down. "There's just one more thing. I'd like you to get the request line up and running full time by next week. I just got the go-ahead yesterday."

"Sure," I said.

"Henry Harkins said he wants the request lines answered seven days a week, from 9:00 a.m. to 9:00 p.m. You'll have to hire at least three more people to answer the phones, one full-time and maybe two or three high school kids part-time. Find some pretty girls. I have some

28

résumés you can look over. One of them is for a girl I'd definitely like you to interview. I got a special call from the New York office about her."

Earl pawed through a few pages on his desk, then pulled out a sheet. "She went to college, so she's a smart kid, and she just moved to the area. Here."

He handed me a résumé with the name Jacqueline Phillips on the top.

"I want you to call her for an interview. She could be helpful to us."

"In what way?"

"She's the daughter of somebody who knows somebody. They specifically asked that we hire her." Earl paused. He looked at me with a hard expression. "It's up to you, of course. But when New York calls..."

"I understand Earl. I'll interview her next week."

I went back to my office and sat down to look at the stack of résumés. I put Jacqueline's on top. She had gone to City University on the East Coast. Right now, she was working as a temporary receptionist for an attorney's office. If she wanted to answer the phones here instead, that was fine with me.

I picked up the phone and dialed.

Jacqueline arrived promptly at five-thirty. I let her in the door at the side of the station. She was a beauty for sure, although she was a little rough around the edges. She had the natural look, without makeup or nail polish. She was wearing a blue flower-print dress with a short hemline. She was petite and young looking, with big blue eyes, and had shoulder-length brown curly hair with blonde highlights. She looked like that girl on cover of the *Blind Faith* album. If she was taller, she could have been a model. As soon as I saw her, I knew I would offer her the job.

She followed me back to my office, and I sat down behind my desk.

"Jacqueline, have a seat."

"I'm glad to meet you, Donnie. And you can call me Jackie."

"I can relate. My real name is Donald, but I go by Donnie."

"Thank you for asking me in for the interview."

"Tell me why you're interested in working in radio, Jackie."

"I have a degree in communications with an emphasis in radio, television, and film. When I was in college, I worked at the college radio station, and I'm doing the same thing here."

"I thought you're doing temp work for a lawyer."

"I am. But when I first got to town, I met the program director of the college station at CSU, and he let me be a disc jockey on Saturday afternoons. It's just for fun—hey don't pay me—but I've made some great friends there."

"I didn't know the local college even had a radio station," I told her. "What kind of songs do they play?"

"The station only broadcasts for five square miles, on and around the campus. They have albums and the station director lets us play what we want. I'm a big fan of the Grateful Dead, Todd Rundgren, Bruce Springsteen, David Bowie, Genesis . . . you know, album rock. But I love Top 40—that's all I used to listen to at home."

"You won't be spinning records at this job," I said. Part of me was laughing at the thought of a girl trying to be a boss jock. "But you'll have plenty to do. And I can hire you full-time. Does that sound like something you'd be interested in?"

"You bet it does!" Then she thought for a second. "How much does the job pay?"

"I'll start you at $3.75 an hour."

"That's not much. It's just to start, right?"

"Yeah. I can probably give you a raise in January, when I get my new budget."

"Okay, that will be fine."

"Great. You're hired. You can start next Monday. I'll give you regular daytime hours, eight-thirty to five-thirty Monday through Friday. That will leave your weekends free for that college station."

"Wow, thank you, Donnie. Thank you so much! That will be perfect."

It was that easy. And hiring the part-timers wasn't much harder. By the end of the week, I had the request line covered twelve hours a day, seven days a week. I found a college dude who desperately wanted to work in radio and two smokin' hot high school chicks who needed after-school jobs. I hoped their daddies would let them go to the station parties.

5

Saturday, September 28, 1974
Billboard Hot 100 Hit Song of the Week:
"Rock Me Gently" by Andy Kim

I decided to throw a "get to know you" gathering for the jocks at my home. I scheduled the event for the last Saturday night in September and quietly spread the word at the station. This was just for me and the jocks, and we were going to do what we wanted, no holds barred. Once Carol and Jason got here, a party like this one would be out of the question.

The new place I had rented was the epitome of California cool. It was the first floor of a beach house with an ocean view, right in the center of the hippest neighborhood in town. From the street, all you saw was the garage, but the living room window gave me my own personal view of the Pacific, 20 feet below. The house was painted pale yellow, to match the other pastel buildings on the block. I don't know what I liked more: the view, the ocean breeze, or the chicks in bikinis walking on the beach. Of course, I missed my Carol, who was still stuck in Houston.

The night of the party arrived. As planned, Patrick Thomas showed up an hour early. Next to Vince, Patrick was my best friend in the world. Patrick was a laid-back

California boy with long, wild, curly reddish hair and a Fu Manchu moustache. Patrick always had a blonde girlfriend and drove a VW van. If he weren't a DJ, he'd probably be a surfer dude.

Patrick also always had pot to share. Every day before his shift, he took a quick drive and came back with red eyes and a cold soda.

As soon as he arrived, he said, "Hey, Donnie, I got some bitchin' Thai stick I've been dying to try. Let's smoke a doobie. We've got almost an hour before the other guys get here."

I didn't need to be talked into it, so we sat on the couch looking out at the ocean and lit up.

"You sure got a great place here," Patrick said admiringly. "This is way better than my pad out by the station."

"And a lot more expensive, too. Turn up the station; let's listen to Sammy."

He moved over to my stereo and upped the volume. Our weekend guy, Sammy Talarico, was blasting Cat Stevens "Another Saturday Night."

I took a long toke. "Man, this is some good shit."

"Yeah, I knew you'd like it. I've been saving it for tonight," he said.

"Thanks," I squeaked as I exhaled. "Do you want a beer?"

"You bet, dude."

I got up to look in the fridge. I only had a few beers left. I brought one to the living room and handed it to Patrick.

"Dude, where's the snacks?" Patrick asked.

"That's partly why I wanted you here an hour early. I need you to head over to the Safeway and pick up some stuff." I handed him two twenty-dollar bills.

"Sure, no problemo. What else do you want?"

I got up and looked in my liquor cabinet in the kitchen. I had vodka, rum, and Jack Daniels.

"Get four six-packs of beer, soda for mixers, some chips, and whatever else you want. I'll order pizza delivery as soon as everyone gets here."

Forty minutes later, Matt West was at the door. "Donnie, dude." Matt pumped my hand and stepped inside. "What's shakin'?" He looked around. "Great place you got here. They must be paying you too much. Where is everyone?"

"Patrick will be right back with snacks and mixers," I said. "Everyone else should be here soon. What can I get you to drink?"

"I'll have a whisky, neat."

I poured him one. He threw it back, and I poured him another.

"Let's talk strategy," he offered. "Nah, on second thought, let's talk about babes. Those new request-line girls are a couple of hot tamales, aren't they?"

"Whoa, dude, aren't you a little old for them?"

"That ain't gonna stop me from lookin'."

A half hour later, everyone else had arrived. Patrick had returned with two grocery bags of snacks and mixers, and I had ordered three large pizzas.

Predictably, after a few tokes and a few drinks, the guys began a heated debate about the hotness of each of the women at the station—and at Harkins Media headquarters. Eventually the discussion turned to Elizabeth Corley, our national music director.

"I'd do her," offered Charlie.

"You horndog, you'd do just about anything in a skirt," I said.

"I'd do her too," Patrick said. "Charlie doesn't just have a boner. He's also got taste."

"Slow down there, rangers," I warned. "That chick belongs to Nick Mitchell."

"That isn't what I heard," offered Patrick. "I heard she likes the ladies."

"Ooh, I'd like to watch that," said Charlie.

I shook my head. "Vince told me she's a force to be reckoned with. You don't want to cross Elizabeth Corley. Trust me, I've heard stories."

"How about those new request line chicks?" Charlie said. "Have you seen that, Jackie? I'd like to jump her bones."

"Shut up! Don't talk about them. They work for me, remember? I've got to look out for those girls."

"What?" Matt half-shouted. "I thought we were here to talk about chicks. I even brought some entertainment. It's in the car."

"Not those dirty movies again," groaned Rex.

"Yeah. Those dirty movies again. New ones." He got up and headed out the door. Fifteen minutes later, he had set up the projector and the film was ready to roll. By then the pizzas arrived, so we filled our plates, and all took seats in the living room.

"Hey Matt, where do you get those films?" asked Charlie.

"None of your damn business," Matt answered. "Just enjoy the show."

"How come you don't have any pictures on the wall?" Keith asked.

"I just moved in, dude. Besides, that's woman's work and my Carol isn't here yet."

"Carol wouldn't like you showing these stag films."

"She's not here, remember?"

The movie was a standard compilation of all sorts of hot chicks giving blowjobs. It started with a naked Swedish blonde. She walked into view, and for a second or two the camera zoomed in on her crotch.

"The carpet matches the drapes," Patrick hollered.

She bent over a long-haired guy who seemed stoned out of his mind, pulled his cock out of his pants, and made him come in less than a minute.

Next on the reel was a German wench wearing only a corset and low-cut blouse. She went about her business with a blond fellow missing his lederhosen.

"Ach du lieber!" gasped Keith from the back of the room.

The film was one blowjob after another, each one performed by a woman from a different country—Italy, Spain, Ethiopia, Japan, and, to everyone's surprise and amusement, Canada. She undressed and blew a guy dressed as a Mountie.

The party wound down soon after the film ended . Everyone splits except Patrick. "Let's hang out for a while longer," he said.

"Yeah, let's talk about the competition and how we're going to crush them."

"Get out the blow, Donnie. I'll roll up the Thai stick."

I went into the bedroom and took out a small vial of coke, then got cozy in the living room. An hour passed as Patrick and I passed around another doobie, argued over our favorite albums, and snorted up a few lines that I laid out on a copy of *Billboard* magazine.

"Hit the volume, dude. Keith Adams is starting his shift and I want to hear how he sounds. I'm not usually up this late."

We listened to his set. Patrick's head bobbed up and down to the beats while Keith played "Sweet Home Alabama," "Beach Baby," and "Nothing from Nothing." At the bottom of the hour, Keith played the station jingle and commercials for a jeans store and McDonald's. Then he made a smooth segue into the next set of songs: "Free Man in Paris," "Jazzman," and "Steppin' Out, Gonna Boogie Tonight."

"Keith really does a great job," Patrick said. "Nobody does the overnight shift better."

"Yeah, he's good," I agreed. "Let's hear what they're playing on 99Z." The Big Z was our main competition in town, and they were known for pilfering our talent. I tuned in the station.

"99Z! 99Z! What's your favorite radio station? 99Z!"

It was a promo from their latest contest, a treasure hunt. They gave clues every day until the lucky winner found the hidden treasure. The winner got $3000, which was small potatoes compared to our contests. The jock's patter was good, though.

"That station really sucks," Patrick said. Then his head began to bob. A minute later he was passed out on the couch, snoring .

I listened a while longer and fiddled around with the radio dial, switching back and forth between our two competitors and us. I made a few mental notes about some of the things I thought Keith could improve on and some of the things I liked or disliked about the other stations.

I ended up smoking the last of the Thai stick by myself. Eventually I wandered back into my bedroom, to dream about my Carol and all the great fun we were going to have in Beach City.

6

Sunday, October 13, 1974
Billboard Hot 100 Hit Song of the Week:
"I Honestly Love You" by Olivia Newton-John

Things were percolating at Beach City. I was getting familiar with the new jocks and staff. The request line was up and running. Life was good.

I spent a lot of my free time with Patrick. We would listen to the station and the competition, smoke a lot of joints, eat a lot of Mexican, and lose money down at the local poker parlor.

Jackie was working out fine as the main request line girl. She came in promptly each morning, put her sandwich in the station fridge, made her cup of tea, and sat in that little room all day, taking requests and dedications. The jocks all said racy things about her behind her back, but they knew not to touch the boss's best girl.

One thing bothered me about her. What was she doing at that college station? Was she giving away any of our station secrets? What did she know and who was she talking to there? Should I even be worried? Or was I being paranoid?

I decided to call Vince in New York for some advice. "Hi, Vince. It's Donnie."

"Dude, how's things on the left coast? You must be a mind reader. I was going to call you today."

"Great, 'cause I've got something to ask you."

"What's up? Are those guys from Groovy Records treating you all right?"

Groovy Records had a few decent artists, but mostly shitty ones. But the owner was in the Organization, so they always got at least one of their songs on the air. Also, envelopes they passed to us always had a nice chunk of cash — usually a Benjamin, sometimes more.

"Yeah, sure. Their promo man flew into town and I got my envelope a couple of days ago. But that's not what I wanted to talk to you about. It's about my new request line chick."

"Funny you should mention her. Jackie, right?"

"Yeah."

"That's what I was going to call you about," Vince said. "Orders just came down from Harkins about her."

"What orders?"

"You and me are going to Las Vegas for a party right after Thanksgiving, and you need to bring some pictures of Jackie."

My heart sank. "For what?"

"You know what."

"I like her. I don't want her involved in anything shady."

"You gotta get over that, dude. Chicks are just chicks. She's nothin' special."

"I still don't like it."

Vince's voice lowered to a growl. "We're not paid to like it. We're paid to do what we're told. You know that. Got it?"

I swallowed. "Got it. But Jackie's why I called you. I don't like what she's doing in her free time."

Vince's voice returned to normal. "What, she's dating a cop or something?"

"Oh, God no—she's a hippie chick. She spends her time at some stupid college station on the weekends."

"So what?"

"I don't know what she's doing there, or what she's telling them about Beach City Top 40. I want to find out."

"Who cares? She's been at Beach City all of a month and all she does is take requests. She doesn't know anything."

"I just don't want her telling other stations about our song rotations, or any of the things we do in programming. Remember, Vince, it's my ass on the line here if she's passing any info."

Vince grunted. "Since it bothers you that much, I know a guy who can check on her. And while he does, he can get some good pictures of her for Vegas. Preferably in a swimsuit."

"I can take some picture of her here at the station." I offered.

Vince said, slowly and emphatically, "Swimsuit." I could hear him flipping through his Rolodex. "Here it is. Kenny Alvarez. I think he's nineteen by now. He can keep an eye on her and get some photos." He gave me a phone number and I scribbled it down.

"Tell Kenny if he does a good job, you'll help him make a professional aircheck and consider him for a weekend DJ job at the station. He's dying to spin records and he has a great radio voice."

"Okay Vince," I said. "I'll call you after I talk to the dude. See you next month in Las Vegas."

"Quit worrying, Donnie. Everything will be fine. If you follow your orders."

was finally beginning to realize what a hard job I had ahead of me. I had to keep on top of everything at the radio station:

the jocks, the music, the promotions, the contests, and the support people. And then there was the whole other layer of intrigue and deception.

There was the usual underhanded radio stuff, like pay for play, and the drugs and gifts from the promo men. Harkins stations were also taking orders from the Organization. That made things really complicated. Every few weeks I had to give the jocks messages to announce over the air, for reasons I didn't even know. And then there was this other part, the part with the girls.

I put that out of my mind and wrote down some notes about what I wanted this Alvarez kid to do for me. Then I dialed his number.

"Hello."

"Hi, is this Kenny Alvarez?"

"Yeah. Who's this?"

"Donnie, from Beach City Top 40. I'm a friend of Vince's."

"Hellooo, Donnie," he intoned, using his best boss jock voice. "What can I do for you?"

"I'd like to meet with you to talk about a little job you might be interested in."

"In radio?"

"Not right away, but it might lead to something down the road."

"Sure, I'm interested." He was trying to sound nonchalant, but I could hear a ting of excitement in his voice.

"When can you meet me?" I asked.

"I'm about to leave for work. I'll be at the gas station from 11:00 to 4:00 today."

"You work at a gas station?"

"Yeah, until I get my break in radio."

"One more thing: are you available on Saturdays?"

"Yeah. Saturday is my day off."

"Good, because the job is on Saturdays. Are you interested?"

"Sure."

"Meet me at 5:00 this afternoon at the Baskin-Robbins in the Beach City mall. I'll be wearing a Rolling Stones t-shirt."

"Um, sure, that will work. I'm wearing a striped t-shirt."

"Okay, see you then."

"Later, man."

At fi o'clock that afternoon, I walked into the ice cream shop. It was almost empty. I was pleased to hear our station playing on the speakers. I scanned the room until I saw a gangly kid wearing a striped t-shirt sitting at a table in the corner. He had straight brown hair down to his collar, parted in the middle, with wispy bangs almost covering his eyes. As I walked closer, I could see that his front teeth were slightly crooked. When he spotted me, he got up and extended his right hand.

"Hey, man, I'm Kenny."

"Great to meet you, dude." I sat down across from him at the little white table.

The next thing he did was slide a cassette across the table – a homemade aircheck.

"I really want you to hear this. I know I'd be perfect for Beach City Top 40. Beach City has been my favorite station since I was a little kid. It's the only station I listen to."

The guy had balls. Good.

"Hold on a minute," I said. "I'm here to talk about a different assignment for you. If you can help me out with this, I'll set you up in the studio and help you make a real, professional aircheck."

He nodded. "I'm listening."

43

"There's a really cute chick that I hired at the station. She answers the request line. I need some background on her."

"Like what?"

"She told me she's a DJ at the CSU college station on Saturdays. I need to find out if she's telling anyone there anything about Beach City Top 40."

Kenny looked at me thoughtfully. "I know a couple of guys at that place. I doubt she's doing much there besides spinning records and talking into the microphone. Besides, they only broadcast on the campus."

I nodded. "I want you to start hanging around up there on Saturdays when she has her shift. Introduce her to your friends and gain her confidence. Then report back to me."

"Okay."

"After a while, once you get to know her better, I want some pictures of her. Preferably in her bathing suit, at the beach or a pool. Got it?"

Kenny squirmed in his seat. "You aren't asking me to do anything illegal, are you?"

"Nah. All I want are some reports of what this chick is up to. And some pictures of her . Nothing funny—no nudes."

Kenny paused for a second, then said, "Sure, I'll do it. What does she look like?"

"She has light brown curly hair and blue eyes. She always wears jeans and a T-shirt and carries a green tapestry hippie bag. You won't have any problem finding her at the college station. She's real cute, but natural. I'll double-check on the time of her shift, but I think it's 2:00 to 6:00 on Saturday. I'll pay you seven dollars an hour. In cash."

I pulled a business card and pen out of my pocket and scribbled my home phone number on the back. "Here's my card. You can use the home number to call me after hours. Is it a deal?"

"It's a deal. But I don't have a camera."

I nodded. "I expected that. I have a camera and some film in my car. I'll get it for you when we leave. When you get the info and the picture, I'll give you a bonus and help you make a real aircheck at the station."

The cassette was still on the table. Kenny said, "Will you take this one for now? Just to hear what I sound like?"

"Sure." I stood up and put it in my jeans pocket. "Now let's go get some ice cream."

We both got up and he reached over the table to shake my hand. He said, "You didn't tell me, Donnie—what's the chick's name?"

I stepped in real close to Kenny and whispered for dramatic effect. "Her name is Jackie."

7

Tuesday, October 29, 1974
Billboard Hot 100 Hit Song of the Week:
"Then Came You" by Dionne Warwick and The Spinners

By late October, I had nicely settled into the job at Beach City. My staff was in place and the station was ready for the fall sweeps. The only person missing was my Carol, still in Houston trying to sell her house.

I got into the office early, a little before 9:00. Matt West was finishing up his shift. Our mid-morning man, Charlie, was hanging out in the kitchen, stirring his coffee, when I popped in.

"Hey, Charlie. How's it hanging?"

"Great, dude—just another day in paradise."

"You got any weekend plans?"

"Nah, just hanging out. Maybe I'll see that movie *Chinatown*. It's at the Cineplex. Did you see it yet? I heard it was good."

I poured a cup of coffee and dropped in two sugar cubes. "Of course it's good, dude. It's got Nicholson and Dunaway. Later." I headed to my office to tackle the pile of mail and messages on my desk.

I looked around the office at how I had personalized the place. I'd stayed late one night with Patrick, and we went to town on the walls with a bunch of colored magic markers. I don't even remember what we were messed up on, but when I got back the next morning I saw wild slogans all over the formerly blank wall: "Right On," "You Gotta Believe," "Groovy," "Shake It Up," "Happy," "Rock and Roll Is Here to Stay," "We're Number One," and "Beach City Top 40 Plays the Hits," scribbled in different colors and all kinds of crazy lettering. I don't know what management thought of it, but as long as the ratings stayed high, I knew I could decorate my office however I wanted.

The phone rang. It was Jenny, Earl Fredrickson's secretary, summoning me into his office, pronto.

I put down my coffee cup and walked through the station. His door was open, and I went right in.

Earl offered his oversized hand and shook mine vigorously. "How are you today, Donnie?"

"Great, dude. Couldn't be better."

"Have a seat, son. I've got some exciting news." He motioned toward the chair facing his desk and walked over to close the door.

"You aren't going to believe this—we've got two of The Beach Boys coming to the station for an interview."

"When?"

"Today. Brian and Dennis Wilson will be coming in at 3:00, escorted by their promo man. Rockin' Rex can interview them. I have an info sheet right here about their latest album and upcoming appearances in our area."

He slid a sheet toward me. It was a press release from Capitol Records with a bunch of information I could use to write out questions for Rockin' Rex's interview.

Then Earl leaned forward over his desk and edged in close. "Our friends from New York want Rex to read a special message on the air at exactly three-thirty today. It's nothing complicated, but I want you to write it out on an index card and make sure Rex knows how important it is."

I sighed. There's always a catch in the radio game.

Earl scribbled some words on a sheet of paper . "Have him read these words, and then have him play the song 'Good Vibrations'".

Earl slid the piece of paper my way. I picked it up. All it said was, *I don't know where, but she sends me there*—a line from the song. It obviously meant something to somebody. I knew better than to ask questions.

"No problem," I said.

Earl leaned back. "Now get out of here and write up those interview questions. Set up the carts of all The Beach Boys songs we have in the studio, so they're ready to play when the guys get here. Close the door on your way out."

I got back to my office and looked at the press release. The Beach Boys had just released a greatest hits album called *Endless Summer*. They were on tour now and had a stadium tour planned for next year with the group Chicago. There was plenty to ask about.

I knew we had at least ten Beach Boys songs on carts in the studio. They were in alphabetical order, so they were easy to find. I left them in a stack for Rex and then called his number.

He answered the call on the second ring. "Rex here."

"Hello, Rex, this is Donnie."

"Hey, man—what's shakin'?"

"We've got a surprise for the listeners today."

"Yeah?"

"You're interviewing two of The Beach Boys live today."

"Ya—hoo!" he answered with his signature yell.

"Get here a little early so we can go over the interview questions."

"Got it, boss."

I was in my office working on the weekly *Hit Sheet* when I heard female squeals coming from the hallway. The Beach Boys had arrived.

I joined the throng as Earl ushered the two stars and their promo man into the control booth. Even Jackie left the request lines to see what the commotion was about.

"Get back to the phones," I told her. "In a few minutes, the lines are going to be on fire." I motioned to the office girls, "The rest of you, stay out of the way, please." Then I pushed into the control booth to watch the interview.

Rockin' Rex had the situation under control. He pulled up two seats for Brian and Dennis Wilson by the microphone and they sat down. Their promo man leaned up against the wall.

As soon as the red light went on, Rockin' Rex began crowing at the top of his lungs. "Hey there, boys and girls, I have surprise guests here at Beach... City... Top... 40—the famous and fabulous Beach boys! They took time from their busy schedule to stop by your favorite... radio... station... Beach... City... Top... 40! I'll be talking with them shortly. First, let's play this song from their newest triple platinum album, *Endless Summer*. We'll be right back with the ... Beach... Boys!"

Then he queued up one of my favorite songs, "California Girls," and made small talk with the guys until the song ended.

"We're back on Beach... City... Top... 40 and I'm talking to Brian and Dennis Wilson from The Beach Boys about their newest triple platinum number one album, *Endless Summer*."

Turning to Dennis, he asked, "What do you think about *Rolling Stone* magazine naming The Beach Boys the number one band of the year?"

"It's wonderful—we're very flattered," Dennis said. His tone was enthusiastic, but I could see in his expression that he'd given the same answer to the same question dozens of times.

Rockin' Rex turned to Brian. "I hear you'll be in our area for three shows very soon."

"Yes."

"How does it feel to be back in sunny California?"

"Our roots are here and it's great to be home." Dennis scratched his forehead. I wasn't sure, but he looked like he was stifling a yawn.

"Dennis, what did you think about your newest album, *Endless Summer*, going triple platinum?"

"We owe it all to the fans, and our favorite fans are from Beach City. Next year we have two more albums coming out."

"Groovy, man," Rockin' Rex said. "And speaking of shows, I heard you're doing a big tour with Chicago next year."

Brian grabbed the microphone. "Yeah, it's going to be a blast! We'll be in Anaheim next May."

Rockin' Rex took back the mike. "Can you dig it, Beach City listeners? An exclusive interview with The Beach Boys and information on a fantastic show next year. Be sure to listen to win. What's your favorite radio station?"

With that, The Beach Boys, Rockin' Rex, me, and the promo man all screamed at the top of our lungs: *"Beach... City... Top... 40!"* Then Rex threw in three carts to play three hits in a row: "Help Me Rhonda," "I Get Around," and "Surfer Girl."

The interview was over. The office staff and jocks were in the hallway outside, crowded around the control booth area. The promo man opened his briefcase and started giving out copies of *Endless Summer* for the artists to sign. He handed me a package of t-shirts that I quickly unwrapped and started passing out, being sure to keep a few for Rockin' Rex and the other jocks.

Suddenly Stephanie came rushing into the hall. "Donnie, there's a riot in the parking lot!"

"What?"

"Yeah, they started showing up as soon as the Beach Boys went on the air."

Our station was off the beaten path, 20 miles east of the city, but a throng of listeners had still driven out here to get a glimpse of the stars as they left.

"Okay, thanks, Stephanie. You lead the way. You can hustle them out the back."

I turned to the promo man. "Go with Stephanie. She'll show you where to bring your car and you can skip out of here."

There was still a crowd of station employees in the hall. They were taking turns chatting up the Beach Boys, getting their records signed, and arguing about their favorite song.

Over the speakers, I could hear that the three-song set was finishing. I looked at the clock through the glass of the control booth. It was 3:29.

First Rockin' Rex played the station ID. Then he announced, "I don't know where, but she sends me there. And here it is, the Beach Boys' number one song, 'Good Vibrations.'"

The visitors had ducked out the back door. People in the office were walking back to their desks.

The excitement was over. Everything had gone as planned and Rockin' Rex had delivered his message without anyone suspecting a thing.

It was just another fun day at Beach City Top 40. But there was always a hidden agenda.

8

Monday, November 11, 1974
Billboard Hot 100 Hit Song of the Week:
"You Ain't Seen Nothing Yet/Free Wheelin'" by Bachman-Turner
Overdrive

K enny checked in with me weekly on his progress with Jackie. The way he talked about her it sounded like he was falling for the chick.

On Monday the 11th, he called me at the appointed time. "Donnie, it's Kenny. Do you have time to talk?"

Jackie was standing in the hall right outside my office, delivering a birthday song request to the control booth. I quickly got up and closed the door.

"Sure. What's goin' on, dude?"

"I have a buddy at the CSU station, a guy named Pete. I know him from high school. His shift is right before Jackie's on Saturday. It was a piece of cake getting in there. It turns out that Jackie and that dude are good friends."

"What did you find out?"

"That girl isn't giving away any secrets. You don't have to worry."

"Are you sure?"

"No one at that college station cares about Top 40 radio. Jackie just grabs the albums and plays the cuts like she's told. The guy who's the program director isn't even around on Saturday."

I let out a long breath. "Good. Listen, Kenny, did you get the shots for me?"

"Yeah, Donnie, I sure did."

"Okay, good. Let's meet at the Baskin-Robbins again and you can tell me everything and give me the film. Can you make it tonight?"

"Yeah, man, I can be there at 6:00."

"Perfect. Later, dude."

I was a few minutes late. Kenny was already at a table, most of the way through an ice cream cone.

I only wanted coffee because I was going to dinner with a record promoter in half an hour. I went to the counter for my java and then joined Kenny. He was wiping the traces of his cone off his fingers.

"Hey, Donnie, have I got a story for you!"

I shook his sticky hand and took a swig of my coffee.

"Not only did I get the pictures, but I nailed her," Kenny said proudly.

I saw a brown grocery bag on the floor by Kenny's foot. "Is that the camera I lent you?"

"Oh, yeah, sure, Donnie. The film is still in there; I hope it turns out okay." He nudged the package in my direction with his foot. "I want to tell you what happened."

I sighed. "Make it quick, Kenny. I've got dinner plans."

"Okay. I came early on Saturday 'cause Pete told me that Jackie might be swimming before her air shift. And when I got there, I saw her '66 Chevy in the parking lot. I walked over to the station and peered in the window and saw Pete on the air, but no sign of Jackie. So, I went to the college pool, and there she was! I got some good shots of her in her swimsuit. She never even saw me."

"Good. How many shots?"

"I don't know, man. Maybe seven or eight. Anyway, when I got back to the station, Pete was still doing his shift. In about twenty minutes, Jackie came in with her hair in ringlets, still wet from the pool. She seemed awful glad to see me."

"What do they play at that rinky-dink station, anyway?"

"Not the hits," Kenny assured me. "They call it free-form, or progressive radio—prog rock for short. The station manager gives everyone a list of songs and the DJs can add a song or two of whatever they want. You know the bands: Genesis, the Rolling Stones, Frank Zappa, Supertramp, Joni Mitchell, Fleetwood Mac, Steely Dan, artists like that. Jackie is a real nut about this guy Todd Rundgren."

"Todd who?"

"I dunno, some guitar player who also produces records. She likes the Grateful Dead, too. You know, she's pretty good on the radio. She's not a boss jock, but she has a really nice radio voice. One day you should put girls on the air."

I raised my eyebrows at that one. But there were a few girl jocks at that hippie station in San Francisco. In radio, anything's possible.

"Oh, one more thing. I got a couple of shots of her at the college station control booth, wearing headsets and spinning records. She looked cute."

I picked up the paper bag. "Thanks, Kenny. You did good. Why don't you meet me next Wednesday night at the station? I'll help you make a real air check and show you how to use the equipment at Beach City. You can give the reel-to-reel to Jackie when you see her next Saturday and ask her to deliver the tape to me. Then she can feel like she helped you get the job."

"Job?"

"Sure, man. If everything goes smoothly and your aircheck is good enough, I'll be able to offer you a weekend gig. I listened to your homemade aircheck."

"You did?"

"Yeah. Since you were so highly recommended by Vince, I thought I'd give it a listen."

"What did you think?"

"I think you have real potential. But I need a real studio aircheck before I decide."

"Thanks, Donnie! That sounds great."

I stood up to leave.

"Wait," Kenny said. "I need to tell you the best part of the story, about Jackie and me getting it on."

"Next time, Kenny. I gotta run now."

I picked up my empty paper cup and threw it in the trash. I had an important dinner with a promo man, and I was hoping to get a little extra money for playing whatever shit he was pushing this week.

9

Wednesday, November 20, 1974
Billboard Hot 100 Hit Song of the Week:
"Whatever Gets You Thru the Night" by John Lennon

I told Kenny to meet me at the radio station at 8:00 p.m., when there would only be a few people around and the production studio would be free. He showed up right on time.

"Hey, man, glad to see you," I said.

"Me too, Donnie."

We went in the side entrance, and I took him on a quick tour of the programming area: my office, Patrick's office, the request booth, and finally the control booth. Patrick flashed us both a big smile. He took off his headsets and let us in.

"Patrick, this is Kenny Alvarez. He's been recommended by Vince, and I'm helping him work on an aircheck tonight."

Patrick extended his hand and shook Kenny's enthusiastically. "Good luck, dude." Then he put his headsets back on and quickly switched the carts to play the next group of commercials and spots.

We stood in the control booth until the next song came on. I motioned Kenny to follow me over to the production studio, shut the door behind us, and sat down in front of the controls.

"I'm going to make it really easy for you," I told him. "All you have to do is talk, and I'll run the board. If you get hired, I'll have my weekend guy, Sammy Talarico, give you more lessons before you go on the air. Right now, I want to hear how tight you are and how you sound."

DJs didn't spin actual records anymore. They just put in the carts, managed the volume controls, and provided the upbeat patter that each jock used to define his radio personality.

I'd brought a bunch of carts into the studio to make the aircheck. The do-or-die part is how a DJ sounds between the songs. One of the most important things every DJ has to learn is how to talk right up to, but not over, the lyrics.

Kenny turned out to be a natural in the studio. I brought in a schedule sheet with the order of the music, promos, commercials, station jingle, and other spots, just like it was a real program. He looked, nodded, and started right in. He had the deep booming boss jock voice and the high energy of a natural DJ. He didn't miss a beat or make a mistake.

When he'd finished, I complimented him on his performance. "Dude, nice job. You did well."

"Thanks," he told me. Then he said, "You know, Donnie, Jackie's a really hot chick."

"Really?" I said, wanting to roll my eyes.

"Uh huh. The afternoon after I took those pictures for you, we went out for some burgers, and then she invited me back to her place. When we got there, she made me listen to Grand Funk Railroad, just because the album was produced by that weirdo Todd Rundgren. She has a thing for him."

"We all have our favorites," I said.

"Then we got super wasted."

"Uh huh."

"First, we played patty-cake in the shower, and then we moved into the bedroom. That chick is smokin' hot."

"Okay, dude, I get the picture. I'm glad you had fun. I don't really give a shit about what you do in private. I just want you to be the best boss jock Beach City Top 40 has ever heard."

"All right, man." Kenny paused. "But there's one thing I want to tell you about her."

"What, man?"

"Her lady parts look weird."

That stopped me cold. "What do you mean?"

"It looks like somebody came after her with a knife. It's all lopsided inside there, like someone cut on it or something."

Christ, these stupid jocks. Does he really think I want an audio tour of my employee's genitals?

"Yeah, you're a lucky dude," I told Kenny. "The girls just fall all over you. Now take a break while I dub this tape for you. Go hang out with Patrick in the control booth. And don't tell anyone else about those pictures you took – or about that night with Jackie. Especially anyone at the station. You know how people gossip."

"Okay, Donnie."

He left, and I bent over the reel-to-reel to splice out the rest of the songs and create a professional-sounding aircheck.

·

Twenty minutes later, came out with a finished tape. I found Kenny in the control room with Patrick. I motioned him to come back into my office, where I handed him the reel.

"Next weekend, when you see Jackie, give her this and tell her to bring it to me. That way, she'll think she helped you get the job."

"Okay, Donnie."

"I'll get back to you in a few weeks, after some of the jocks hear your audition tape and I get the approval to hire you."

Kenny beamed.

"Now, this isn't just about becoming a DJ," I said. "You're also going to be my go-to boy for keeping an eye on that chick. Just be nice to her and tell me whenever you see or hear anything about her that I might want to know."

"No problemo," Kenny said.

I walked him to the door and watched him cross the parking lot to his beat-up car. He didn't look like much, but that kid had something. He could go far in radio, if he was smart enough not to screw things up.

10

Wednesday, November 27, 1974
Billboard Hot 100 Hit Song of the Week:
"I Can Help" by Billy Swan

B y the end of November, things were smooth as silk at Beach City Top 40. Ratings were high, revenue was strong, and morale was good.

I had some things to discuss with Patrick, so I asked him to come to work half an hour before his 6:00 p.m. shift.

Patrick popped his shaggy mane into my office doorway. "How's it hanging, dude?"

"Come on in."

Patrick sprawled out on a sofa facing my desk. "What's up?"

"I want to go over the schedule for the weekend, since I'll be in Vegas with Vince, and you'll be running the show."

"Yeah, dude. Too bad you can't be with your old lady."

"I know. At least I'll see her for Christmas. She's having a hard time selling her place in Houston. Interest rates are almost 10 percent. It's crazy."

"That's a bummer. Bet you can't wait for her to get here."

"No kidding." I handed him a sheet of paper. "Here's the full rundown for the weekend . Look it over and let me know if there's anything that looks like you can't handle."

Patrick scanned the page quickly. "It's all good. Don't worry, man. Everything will be fine while you're gone. It's only for a couple of days."

I leaned forward and pointed at his chest. "Listen, Patrick, I have a note here for you to read on the air tonight exactly at 8:01, after the station jingle."

"Pass it over."

I gave the note to Patrick. It used the title of one of the current hit songs to send an Organization message. All it said was *"You Ain't Seen Nothin' Yet" on Beach City Top 40*. I had no idea what that meant, and I didn't care. And I wasn't so dumb as to ask about it.

"Am I supposed to say this and then play the song?"

"Yeah. The song is part of the message. I think another song would mean something else."

"Consider it done."

"Good." I started to stand up.

"Donnie," Patrick said, "wait a sec—I need to shut the door." He got up and closed my office door. "I want to ask about some of the rumors I've heard."

I sat back down. "Rumors? What rumors?"

"I'm talking about girls." He lowered his voice to a whisper. "You and Vince aren't messing around with the station girls, are you?"

"What—you mean, like, screwing them?"

Patrick shook his head. "No. I mean, like, pimping them out. I've heard that sometimes the girls at the station parties might not want to be there."

I laughed. "When we have girls at our parties, those girls *definitely* want to be there. They all want to party with DJs. You of all people should know that."

Patrick frowned. "I've heard rumors about Jackie. I'm beginning to really like her—she's a good kid. I just wanted to make sure everything was on the up-and-up."

"Nothing is going on with Jackie, Patrick. I know she's your friend. In fact, I have something good to tell you about Jackie."

"Yeah?"

"I really like the job she's been doing, and since she's working out so well, I'm going to promote her after the first of the year. I'm going to make her my secretary and your assistant music director."

Patrick's expression brightened. "No kidding!"

"Yeah. So don't worry about her. Nothing bad is going to happen to her. I've got my eye on that kid." *You bet I do*, I thought.

11

Friday, November 29, 1974
Billboard Hot 100 Hit Song of the Week:
"I Can Help" by Billy Swan

The big event was planned for the Saturday after Thanksgiving.

On turkey day, I gave Rockin' Rex the afternoon off so he could be with his girl, and I took his shift. Then, at 6:00, I left the station and drove over to Rex's place for my plate of food and fixings.

The dinner was good, but I was more excited about my upcoming weekend in Vegas. Without Carol and Jason, Thanksgiving didn't mean that much to me.

On Friday at four-thirty I called Patrick into my office. "I'm leaving for Vegas in about an hour; you got any questions?"

"No, man. Quit worrying. Everything will be fine."

I wrote down the name of my hotel and slid it across the desk to him . "Here's where you can reach me."

"Is this another one of those programmers' meeting"

"Uh huh. Vince is flying in from New York. He's probably in the air right now."

"Be sure you have plenty of gas and soda for your ride," cautioned Patrick. "You'll be driving through Death Valley."

"I'll be fine. I just had the Camaro serviced." I stood up. "All right, dude. As of five-thirty, you're the boss man," I said. "Don't do anything I wouldn't do."

"Okay," Patrick replied. "Later, man."

"Later," I answered, as I ducked out the door.

As soon as I arrived, I called Vince from the lobby. Nick Mitchell at Harkins Media told us that we were going to share a room. I didn't really mind since it was with Vince and was only for two nights.

It was a nice room, with a well-stocked mini-bar, two double beds, a couch and a coffee table. I walked over to the large windows and gazed out at the great view of the city lights.

Vince joined me at the window, nodding approvingly. Then he drew shut the curtains. "Dude, you brought your stash, right?"

"Let me get it out." I unzipped my duffel and pulled out my coke and pot. "You go ahead, I'm gonna hop in the shower."

I went into the bathroom, hoping Vince wouldn't snort up the weekend's stash in the first hour.

It was almost 11:00 by the time I was ready. I sat down next to Vince to snort a few lines and roll up a joint. I wanted to work up a real appetite before we headed down to the 24-hour buffet.

"Put this wet towel in the crack of the door," I said, grabbing one from the bathroom and handing it to him . He did as I asked and sat back down next to me.

I lit the doob, took a long drag, and passed it over to my friend.

He took it. "You've got the pictures of the girl?"

"Yeah, of course."

"Let me see."

"Okay." I took the pictures out of my duffel and showed them to Vince. They were the best of the ones Kenny had taken at the college swimming pool. Jackie was wearing a red two-piece bathing suit.

"Oh, perfect. The horndogs from East Dipshit, New Jersey are going to love this little lady."

After pigging out at the buffet, we stood at the entrance to the casino, stomachs full, nicely buzzed.

"Donnie, what do you think about a little fun for tonight?" Vince said.

"Sure, dude," I said. "Let's do it."

As soon as we hit the casino floor, a chick walked up to us—a blonde in a short black skirt and a sequined halter top.

"Me and my girlfriend want to party," she whispered in my ear. She was a shapely girl, but her breath stunk of liquor. "Are you interested?" She pointed behind Vince.

Both of us turned and saw the second chick. She was a skinny brunette who seemed out of it. Vince grabbed her arm, drew her closer, and smacked her on the ass. "Do you girls know who we are?" he half shouted.

The brunette shook her head.

"We're the kings of rock and roll."

"You don't look like rock stars to me," she mumbled.

"We *make* the stars!" said Vince. Then, grabbing the brunette's arm and drawing her toward him, he asked. "How much for a party?" She bent down, revealing her cleavage, then stood back up and whispered something in his ear.

"A hundred bucks! That's too much. I'll give you fifty."

"Keep your voice down, dude," I said.

The brunette mouthed "yes," and the blonde nodded in agreement.

We all headed toward the elevator, the brunette staggering a little on her platform heels. Vince pressed the elevator button, and we went upstairs.

When we got to the room, the blonde walked over to the window, stuck her head through the closed drapes, and peered at the night sky above the Nevada desert. Then she pulled her head back and sat down on the bed in anticipation.

"This sure is a pretty room," she said. "You guys must be VIPs or something."

"Yeah," I said. "I told you, we're the kings of rock and roll. And the barons of the blues."

The girls giggled in response.

I pulled the baggie and a razor blade out of my dopp kit and put out four lines of coke on the glass-topped coffee table. Then I rolled up a twenty from my wallet and the four of us took turns snorting up the coke.

"Let's see the money," whispered the brunette.

Vince pulled out his leather wallet and paid the girls. Now the party could really begin.

Immediately, the two girls took off their tops. They did a little shimmy, shaking their tits, and pulled back the bedcovers. The whole performance was obviously choreographed—these two clearly worked together—but I didn't care.

The blonde went over to sit on my lap and started to pull up my t-shirt. Vince grabbed some beers from the mini-bar and pulled out a joint.

We were sloppy, high, and drunk, but the girls still knew what to do. The brunette unzipped Vince's pants and the blonde worked on my cock, her lips expertly sucking it up and down. Then they led us over to the beds and we all got down to business.

When I woke up on Saturday, it was almost noon. My head was spinning. I got up to take a piss and saw that Vince was already drinking coffee and smoking a cig.

I was a lot more worn out from the drive and the partying than I figured. We took turns showering and shaving, and we made it down to the buffet just before it switched to lunch.

There wasn't much conversation. I knew tonight would be a long night, so I needed to conserve my energy, and my drugs.

"Let's just play poker this afternoon, Vince."

"Sure. That'll pass the time."

We headed over to the casino floor. The poker table wasn't crowded, and it was easy for me to win. I was usually lucky at cards. By 2:45 I was up about 150 bucks.

Vince didn't do as well; he was down over 200, so he decided to quit and go back up to the room.

After a couple of hours, I joined him, and we called room service for some dinner. The waiter brought our food and set it up on the same glass-topped coffee table we'd done lines off of the night before. Vince was the tired one now; he dozed off for a bit after dinner on the couch.

At 9:00 p.m. I shook him awake. "Get up, Mr. National Program Director," I said. I was wired and ready. "Time for the big event."

"All right, I'm up." He stumbled into the bathroom to brush his teeth.

At 10:00 we got on the casino elevator and pressed the button for the penthouse. A minute later, we got off and looked around. The entryway looked like something from Liberace's house.

"I don't think we're dressed right for this," I said, looking down at my jeans and sneakers.

"Screw 'em," said Vince.

A tall guy in a suit was guarding the door. He looked us up and down. His gaze was not friendly. "Are you sure you boys are in the right place?"

"Yeah," Vince said. "We're two of the radio guys; check your list. Vince Johnson and Donald Dixon."

"Wait right here," he instructed. He opened the door and walked through the doorway. A few seconds later he came back out and motioned for us to follow him inside.

We walked into a small area that led into the main meeting room. A slight but well-dressed man was sitting at a table looking at sheets of names. He looked down at his list and found us. I peeked around him and saw the larger room filled with tables and men, some milling around, drinks in hand, others seated and eating. I smelled cigar smoke.

A huge middle-aged man in a black suit walked into the area where we were standing and whispered into the ear of the guy behind the table. The man at the table said, "Donnie, Vince, this is Albert. Tonight, you may hear some people address him as Big Al."

That wasn't an exaggeration. The guy was easily 300 pounds. He was dressed in classic Organization attire: thick gold chains, star sapphire pinky ring, and custom suit.

"Good to meet you, man," I said, thrusting out my hand toward him.

He enthusiastically shook my hand. "This is Giorgio, my right-hand man." He pointed to the man who had led us inside.

"Nice to meet you, dude."

Giorgio didn't take my hand. He gave me a curt nod. Then he excused himself and returned to his post by the door.

Big Al looked us over in our t-shirts, jeans, and sneakers; then he put his arm around me and walked me further into the room. Vince walked in behind us and went over to the bar.

"Donnie, next time bring a tie, okey dokey?"

"Sorry, Al. I didn't know it was formal."

"You radio dudes are a bunch of slobs. But I'm glad you could join us."

Al reached into his pocket and pulled out his bankroll. "Here's a couple of bucks for a good time while you're here." He pressed a hundred-dollar bill in my hand. "I hope you've got something good for me."

I said, "I do, Al. She's a doll, a living doll. She'll make plenty for you."

"Have you done her yet?"

Shit. "Not yet," I replied. "But I will."

"All right." Big Al said. "Let's join the party." He led the way into the next room.

Altogether, there were about 40 men in the room. Some were from the Organization, dandied up in expensive suits. Others, like Vince and me, were dressed in jeans and T-shirts, and just as obviously represented radio. A few others wore fancy suits but looked completely different than Big Al's group. They didn't wear Rolexes and thick gold chains. Their clothes were discreet rather than flashy.

Big Al saw me looking at them and said, "Those guys are aides to two senators." He patted me on the shoulder. "Enjoy yourself, Donald." Then he moved off to mingle with the other guests.

Vince walked over to me, whiskey in hand. "Whaddya think, Donnie?"

"I think we're out of our league," I said. "But we've got something they want."

"We certainly do. Listen, I've met Big Al once before."

"Yeah?"

"Yeah, in Manhattan . He took me to a restaurant hidden behind a ladies' lingerie shop. Best Italian I ever had."

71

"Nice."

"Donnie, I'll be back in a minute. I just spotted an old buddy of mine." A moment later he was gone.

The guests were milling around a couple of large tables, drinks in hand, talking and scarfing hors d'oeuvre from the buffet. A few were smoking cigars. I pulled out a cigarette and nervously puffed on it for a minute, then stubbed it out in an ashtray. I spied an empty table and sat down.

A minute later, I spotted Vince heading toward me. He was with two other radio men, and he had his arm around one guy's shoulder.

"Donnie, this is Rich Reid. He's the general manager of a Top 40 station in Tampa."

"Great to meet you, dude," I said.

"Me, too," Rich answered. "I've read all about Beach City Top 40. Bartell Media does the best contests."

"Thanks, man." I nervously fingered the edges of the pictures in my pockets. I knew that there were other men in the room with pictures, too. I said to Rich, "Are you here to buy or sell?"

"Buy," Rich said. "And you?"

"Sell. Is this your first time here?"

"Yeah. It's my first time in Vegas."

"Me, too," I said. "Do you like it?"

"Love it. How about you?"

"It's okay. You know, win a little, lose it back."

I saw Big Al walk to the front of the room. He looked at the crowd and said in a loud voice, "Gentlemen, take your seats."

Six round tables had been set up, each one surrounded by six chairs. Each table had ashtrays, glasses, and a pitcher of cold water in the center.

Slowly, the men took seats around the tables. It was getting warm in the room, and some of the men loosened their ties as they made themselves comfortable. Vince, Rich, and I joined a trio of other radio guys at a table near the back of the room.

Big Al smiled. "We all know why we're here, gentlemen, and I'd like to thank each and every one of you for coming out to Las Vegas this weekend. I'd also like to welcome my new friends from radio stations in Southern California, New Orleans, and Tampa."

The men applauded politely.

Al went on: "To our other friends from all over the country, thanks for making it, guys. Be sure to tell the little ladies we're sorry to take you away from your families on Thanksgiving weekend for our important business. They're probably glad to get rid of you so they can go shopping."

That got a laugh.

"I heard we have some lovely merchandise to look at. My trusted associate Giorgio will keep track of your bids." Big Al paused and let his gaze rove among the tables. "Let the auction begin!"

Giorgio made his way from table to table, collecting photos from sellers, then taping them to sheets of cardboard with lines for writing down bids. When he reached me, I passed my pictures of Jackie to him.

It wasn't like a farm auction with an auctioneer. It was a silent auction. Giorgio passed around the five sheets of cardboard. If a guy liked what he saw, he wrote down a bid. If another guy wanted the merchandise, he put a higher bid underneath.

The men passed around the pictures, sweating and pointing. Soon they were taking off their jackets and rolling up their sleeves. They poured themselves water to go along with their drinks and craned their necks in the direction of the photos as they went around the tables. Big Al watched it all appreciatively from the front of the room.

Across the table from me, Rich chided the man next to him. "Is that all you're going to bid?" he said when the guy wrote an amount underneath the picture of a gorgeous blonde.

"There's a premium for gingers," said one of the Organization guys at the next table. I looked over. He was eyeing a picture of a busty redhead who couldn't have been older than eighteen.

These Organization men knew what they wanted. Judging from their high-end suits, gold jewelry, and expensive watches, these were men who liked attractive things. It didn't matter that some of them had daughters the same age. These were men who just took—or bought—whatever they wanted.

Vince leaned toward me. "Harkins is gonna make a lot of money off Jackie," he assured me. "And so are you and me. What are you going to do with your share?"

"I'm going to buy something really nice for Carol. Maybe a diamond pendant to go with her wedding ring."

She'll like that."

Eventually the ashtrays were filled to overflowing, and the water pitchers were empty.

"Final bid, gentlemen, final bid!" Big Al announced. Giorgio scurried around all the tables and gathered up the pictures.

"I have an announcement to make," Al said, smiling broadly.

"What now?" yelled a guy from the back.

"I'm going to let the *two* highest bids on each girl win. That means double the number of lucky winners. You can decide on delivery later. Just be sure to pay your 20% deposits before you leave. You know the rules: if you can't pay the 20% now, the girl goes to the next bidder down the list."

I searched for another glass of cold water. I couldn't find one, so I lit up another cig.

I watched some of the guys pull out their billfolds and go up to Big Al's table to settle. I sat in the back with Vince until it was all finished and Giorgio told us that Al was ready to see us.

We walked to the front of the room. As soon as Big Al saw me, he beamed. "We did really good tonight, Donnie; your chick is Miss Popularity."

"Yeah, I bet. What do I do next?"

"There are going to be two parties for your little honeypot. One will be in January in Palm Springs, with some really important people. The second will be for one of the radio men; we'll do something at the radio convention in San Francisco. I'll give instructions to Harkins, and he'll have someone contact you."

By now, I had had enough. All I wanted to do was smoke some pot and crawl into bed. "So, is that it?" I asked.

"Yeah, that's it." Big Al leaned toward me with a small sneer. "No, one more thing. Those photos you took of Miss Popularity—I'm keeping them."

I shrugged. "Sure."

"And remember—next time, wear coats and ties. Good night gentlemen."

That was the end of our big evening.

Vince and I went back to our room. I took a shower and dropped into bed, exhausted.

Monday morning, I was back at work. No one suspected a thing. As far as they knew, Thanksgiving weekend had been nothing but a turkey dinner and football games.

12

Friday, December 20, 1974
Billboard Hot 100 Hit Song of the Week:
"Kung Fu Fighting" by Carl Douglas

The Friday before Christmas, we had a little holiday party at the station. Earl Fredrickson provided lunch for the whole staff, with platters of sandwiches, chips, and cookies. The office girls decorated the place with tinsel, lights, and a miniature Christmas tree.

It was nice of Earl to do this. And I was glad it was held on Friday because I was finally leaving on Sunday to visit Carol in Houston. I couldn't wait to see her. We talked almost every night on the phone, but that only made me miss her more. I kept urging her to drop the price on the house, but she wanted to hold out for every last penny. I think she felt that her ex owed her.

When I got to the party, Rex and Stephanie were chatting with some of the office girls. James Ryan was talking to Jackie about the weekly *Hit Sheet*, and Sammy Talarico and Keith Adams were filling their plates. Earl and the sales team weren't around—their own holiday lunch was probably at a ritzy restaurant. I nibbled on a handful of peanuts and gulped down a soda, waiting for Patrick.

Finally, at about 12:45, Patrick arrived. He came over to where I was sitting and pulled up a chair right next to me.

"Patrick, dude, I've been waiting for you."

"Hi, Donnie, Merry Christmas. I hear you're going to celebrate the birth of Jesus with some long overdue you-know-what. When's your flight to Houston?"

"It's Sunday morning. I'm already packed."

"What did you get for Carol?"

"It's sparkly and it's in a small box."

"Come on, tell me."

"It's a pendant to match her ring."

"She'll love it," Patrick said. "How 'bout the kid?"

"I'll get him something when I get there. Carol will help me pick out some stuff at the toy store. Listen, remember that aircheck I played for you?"

"That Alvarez guy, right? He's good. We'll need a Sunday morning guy starting in January, won't we?"

"Yeah, we will," I said.

"Then you should hire him. But have him dump the Hispanic name. Kenny Alvarez doesn't exactly roll off the tongue. Make him Kenny King or something."

"Kenny King. It's great. I'll call him on Monday."

13

Monday, January 6, 1975
Billboard Hot 100 Hit Song of the Week:
"Lucy in the Sky with Diamonds" by Elton John

After New Year's, I figured it was time to promote Jackie. Although I'd hired her to answer the request line, I knew she was capable of a lot more. She never made mistakes, she worked hard, and she certainly was pretty.

On the first Monday of the new year, I called her into my office. Just as she sat down, Rod Stewart's "Maggie May" came on the radio . That was no surprise: our mid-morning man Charlie Greene was a total Stewart fan.

"Do you like that song?" Jackie asked. "I saw Rod Stewart in concert when I was in college."

"He's fine. Listen, Jackie, I want to talk to you about something important. You've done a great job with the request line. I'd like to promote you to be my secretary and assistant music director to Patrick Thomas."

Her whole face lit up. "Cool! When do I start... and I get a raise, don't I?"

"You do. You can start next week, and I think we can give you an extra fifty cents an hour. Plus, you'll get free records, t-shirts, and concert tickets." It wasn't like the station paid for any of these, but a perk's a perk.

"What will my duties be?"

"Mostly I need you to answer the phone and fend off some of the record promoters. You can open my mail, file my papers, keep the records in order—you know, general secretary stuff."

"I can do that. I've been a secretary in a law office."

"This job will be a lot more fun," I promised.

"Where will I work?"

"You can share an office with Patrick. There's a big desk in there, and he doesn't come in until late in the day anyway."

"That will work out. Me and Patrick get along really good, you know?"

"Yeah, I know; he likes you."

Jackie made a face. "No, he doesn't."

"Not like that. As a friend."

"Um, right."

"Then it's settled. I'll get the paperwork going and have you promoted as of next Monday. A new job for a new year. Congratulations."

"Thank you, Donnie!" She looked like a kid who'd just gotten a pile of Christmas presents.

"One more thing," I said. "You know the *Hit Sheet* we print once a week. How would you like to take photos for it? I know you have a Minolta; I've seen it."

"Yeah, I love to take pictures." She paused for a moment. "As long as the station pays for the film and developing."

"I'll reimburse you from petty cash." I stood up. "Now go get some more tea and get back to the request lines."

"Okay, Donnie. Thanks again. I can't wait to start."

It was settled. Jackie was going to take pictures, saving me a bundle on professional photography. She'd answer all of my annoying phone calls, keep things organized for me, and help out Patrick. I would have more time for other things, and Patrick would have more time to produce commercials and jingles.

Things were working out well with this pretty girl.

14

Saturday, January 11, 1975
Billboard Hot 100 Hit Song of the Week:
"Lucy in the Sky with Diamonds" by Elton John

I was invited to a special Harkins Media conference held right here in Southern California on the second weekend in January. All the bigwigs from New York, and all the program and music directors from Harkins stations, would be there. It was being held at the Capri Island Hotel, a highly exclusive hotel and event center. This place was so fancy you could only get to it one way—over a toll bridge that kept the riffraff off the island.

I had never been to a conference like this, so I didn't really know what to expect. But I was happy I would get to hang out with Vince again.

The featured guest was Ben Bailey, the former program director for Beach City Radio, who now ran his own research company. Our station was one of his clients. Ben had an invention—a ratings analysis program that he called simply "the book." This meeting was all about training us to use it. The event ran all day Saturday, and I'd heard from Vince that something special was planned for Saturday night.

When I got to the conference room on Saturday morning, Vince was literally the first person I saw. There he was with his long hair tied back into a ponytail, wearing a blue T-shirt with a surfboard printed on it.

"Man, how ya doin'?" He grabbed my hand and shook it vigorously.

"Long time no see," I said.

"How's the little lady?"

"She's still in Houston."

I smelled alcohol on his breath. Vince must have hit the mini bar before breakfast.

"Are you happy at Beach City Top 40?" he asked. "Don't you just love it?"

"It's bitchin'. Best station ever."

"I've been listening—it sounds great. Hey, I bet there's some guys here you don't know. I'll introduce you..."

He took my arm and started walking me around the room. One by one, he introduced me to some of the other guys from Harkins stations around the country.

Then we grabbed some coffee and took our seats. A minute later, Henry Harkins, Elizabeth Corley, and Nick Mitchell appeared. They said hello, shook our hands quickly, and sat across the table from us. The other station guys sat at other round tables, sipping their coffee and munching donuts. All eyes were on Ben and his partner Lou Arnold as they took their places.

Ben Bailey was as close to a genius as anybody I'd ever met in radio. He brought Beach City Top 40 to number one in our entire market, and it had stayed there for the past five years. The numbers of the other Harkins stations were getting better, too. His research company, WKR Radio Research, used the latest technology—computers. He and Lou had figured out a scientific way to make sense out of the stats from the Arbitron ratings. Their book was a new-fangled way to game the system—all perfectly legally.

For years, Arbitron ratings had decided whether a station lived or died. The company sent out paper diaries to randomly selected households during the ratings sweeps. Each person in the household over age 16 got their own diary. They were instructed to write down every radio station they listened to and to note whenever they turned each station on or off.

After a month, the households sent their diaries back to Arbitron, where the information was compiled and categorized. Even a half a percentage point could change the income of a station for a year, because advertisers purchased airtime depending on the results of those ratings.

Ben had brought large boxes of sample ratings books for everyone in the room. As he and Lou passed them out, the room hushed, like they were handing out bibles. I quickly opened my own copy. It was brief—about fifty pages.

When the books were all distributed, Ben began. "I'm Ben Bailey, and this is my partner Lou Arnold, from WKR Radio Research. Today, we're introducing our latest innovation—the book that will revolutionize your radio station and put you on top."

The crowd gave Ben a loud round of applause.

Lou said, "You have in your hands a sample research book, and today we're going to explain how to use it. Starting in February, each one of you will be getting personalized books that we'll send directly to your station every other month. We'll to show you how to use these books to destroy your competition and become number one in your market."

More loud clapping.

Ben said, "For each competitor in your market, we'll provide detailed comparisons with your station, in columns. Open your sample books to page five and you can see what I mean."

Pages rustled as the men turned to the right page.

"Then we break down our listener patterns by categories. Now turn to page 12 and you'll see how we do this."

Pages rustled again.

"Male and female, ages, and hours of the day. For our purposes, we're only interested in ages 16 to 24, 25 to 36, and 36 to 49. Anyone older than that isn't really of much use to us or our advertisers."

Lou said, "Our ratings are also determined by how long each person listens and when they turn off the radio or change to another station. If you look at page 20 of your books, you can see how we break this down." More rustling. "For example, on this page you'll see that men aged 25 to 49 are listening in their cars from six to seven-thirty in the morning, and from four-thirty to six on their way home from work. The trick is to get them to keep their radios on, at work and at home."

I did my best to follow along, but Ben and Lou weren't great presenters. It was clear that they were statisticians as much as they were radio men.

I knew how important this all was to our stations, but the truth was that I was bored. I quickly got the basic idea: to take all the statistics in the book and tweak each broadcast to get the right demographic to listen just a little bit longer.

Eventually Ben and Lou finished their speech and received thunderous applause. Then Henry Harkins himself took the stage, smiling like a beauty pageant host.

"Thanks, everyone. As you know, I've been in the radio business for many years. I started in my home state of Michigan and built up this chain station by station: investing, upgrading, and investing again. We've sent in our own teams, fixing problems, increasing power, building new studios, and hiring the best. The best station managers, the best sales teams, and the best overall talent in the business. And now all our hard work, yours and mine, is going to pay off. We're going to turn the numbers from these new ratings books into gold with the best contests in radio. I've got plans to give away more cash, cars, and prizes than ever before. And each one of you will be able to proudly say, 'I work for Harkins Media, the best radio chain in the U.S.A.'"

The audience jumped to their feet and applauded. I followed suit, of course.

"You can have faith in Ben's research," Harkins said, "And remember, in our markets it's our proprietary information—ours and ours alone. We've spent a ton—no, several tons—of money on this research, and on ensuring that WKR provides it to us and only us. Breathe a word of any of it to anyone outside of our company, and your career at Harkins media will be over."

Harkins' smile disappeared. For a second or two, he just glared at us.

Then the smile returned. "You'll get your own WKR books about a month after the ratings end in March, and then every other month after that. Ben will be available to go over all your numbers, to help you strategize for your individual stations. I have confidence in him, and so should you. So." The smile disappeared again. "Do. Your. Jobs."

Harkins returned the mike to Ben and sat back in his seat.

"Gentlemen, and ladies," Ben said, nodding in Elizabeth's direction, "I have a major surprise for you. Tonight, we're all invited to a special private concert back here in this room. Our friends at MGM records have graciously invited their number one star, Gloria Gaynor, to sing a few songs for our group before her big concert tomorrow in Los Angeles. She's driving here with her keyboard player for this special treat. I'll see everyone back here at 8:00 p.m.

sharp. Meanwhile, go enjoy the rest of the day at the Capri Island Hotel." Another round of applause burst forth, then slowly died down.

As Vince and I stood up. I felt a hand on my arm.

I turned. The hand belonged to Nick Mitchell, the executive vice president of Harkins Media and Henry Harkins' second in command. His other hand was squeezing Vince's shoulder.

"Donnie, I have something important to discuss with you. Vince, I need you too."

Vince and I looked at each other.

"Let's go to my room right now," Nick said. "It won't take long."

It didn't surprise me that Nick had an entire suite on the top floor to himself. He gestured for us to take seats in the plush club chairs in the corner. I sat, then quickly looked out the window, scanning the pool below and the brilliant blue of the ocean just beyond.

Nick stood before us in his suit, looking like a TV news anchor who was about to announce the lead story of the night.

"Donnie, I brought you up here to explain how things are going to go down. Now that you're one of our program directors, you need to be trained in for your duties outside the station. Vince knows the drill, so you can go to him if you have any questions or problems."

That didn't sound good, but what could I do but listen? I pulled my pack of smokes out of my jeans.

"You don't mind if I smoke, do you, Nick?"

"Smoke away," Nick said, but the expression on his face was deeply serious. "Now listen. This is about the girl at your station. Jackie. She's going to be the first. And here's the good news. We have a new way to make sure the girls don't remember anything. It's a pill that we got from one of our most important clients."

A deep hole opened in the bottom of my stomach. "Wait," I said. "What exactly are you asking me to do?"

"Don't ask too many questions, man," Nick said sharply. "This client is from the military. At a very high level." He paused. "And Donnie, let me be clear—I'm not *asking*. I'm *describing* your duties. Fulfilling them is a condition of your continued employment at Harkins Media. Got that?"

I coughed hard, but I managed to nod.

"Okay. When there's a party, and when we tell you to, it's your job to bring the girl. Jackie is the first. There will be others later. Sometimes you'll do the drugging; sometimes that task will be assigned to someone else. When you're the point person, I'll make sure you get the pills in advance. You smash them up and put them in whatever the girl is drinking. If she doesn't like booze, put them in her soda. You give each chick one dose in advance and a second dose as soon as she wakes up, after the festivities are over. The second dose is to make sure she doesn't remember anything. Then you get her back home and tuck her in bed."

I didn't say anything. I looked at my hands to make sure they weren't trembling. They weren't, thank God.

Nick smiled. "Donnie. Do your job well and we're going to make you one of us. You have the potential to go far with this company."

I finally found my voice. "But Jackie…she's got a college degree. Why her ? She isn't just some chick from the street."

"That makes our clients want her even more—and pay more for her. And don't worry, you'll get your turn, too."

I felt the blood drain from my face. The hole in my stomach expanded.

Nick placed his hand lightly on my shoulder. "Donnie, you're a smart guy. You'll get the hang of it really quickly. And with these new drugs, there are never any problems. Never."

I couldn't stop myself. I turned to Vince and looked straight into his eyes. He shrugged and motioned me to look back at Nick.

"There's one more thing," Nick said. "Tonight, Elizabeth is going to do a special ritual, just after midnight. Both of you need to be there. Room 441. Exactly at midnight."

I was starting to feel dizzy. "A ritual? What kind of ritual?"

"You'll see. And don't be surprised; a few other people you know will be there. We invited that new jock of yours, Kenny. We want to make sure he's on board with our program."

I knew my mouth was hanging open. "*Kenny?* What do you want with Kenny?"

Nick just shook his head. "That's all for now, Donnie. Mr. Harkins and I are counting on you."

Vince and I got up and we shook hands with Nick. My heart was pounding, and I was sweating up a storm. All I wanted was to get out of that hotel room. I needed to take a shower, smoke some pot, and think about what I was going to do.

It was almost midnight. The conference and the concert were over. Vince and Kenny stood behind me as I knocked on the door to 441. Elizabeth opened it and silently motioned us inside. The curtains were tightly drawn and the only light in the room was from a single lamp, dimmed by a scarf over the shade. As soon as my eyes adjusted, I saw the place was set up like Halloween—except this was for real. Three other men I had met at the conference were there too, standing silently.

Elizabeth was wearing a long, flowing robe and black boots. Big silver hoops dangled from her ears. Her hair was brushed back and slicked down. For a moment she stood in front of us, spreading out her arms. Then she moved them around rhythmically, as if she were dancing to music that only she could hear. I caught a whiff of exotic, musky perfume.

Elizabeth had pushed all the furniture out of the way and put a big black cloth in the middle of the floor. Candles placed on tall candleholders were lit in the four corners of the room. I could see and smell incense burning on the dressers and nightstands.

The edges of the cloth on the floor were embroidered with unusual symbols. Using thick chalk, Elizabeth had drawn a large circle on the cloth, and a triangle in the center of the circle.

In the middle of the triangle sat a small table covered with another embroidered black cloth. On the table were a wand, a dagger, a bottle, a chalice, and a book—and next to the book was one of the pictures of Jackie that Big Al had insisted on keeping.

Elizabeth wore a large silver ring on the middle finger of her manicured left hand. It highlighted her blood-red nails. I looked a little closer at the ring. It was engraved with a five-pointed star, with a dark red garnet in the center. There were cryptic letters around the edges.

This chick was a witch. I was fascinated and repulsed at the same time. And I was terrified. What had I gotten myself into?

The three of us just stood there, not knowing what to do.

Finally, Elizabeth spoke. "Take your places," she said, jabbing her finger toward each of the three points of the triangle. Then she walked over to the lamp and turned it off.

Now the candles illuminated the room. The strong smell of incense was starting to give me a headache.

Back against the window, just in front of the drawn curtains, stood the three other guys from a different Harkins station. Counting Elizabeth, there were seven of us.

Pointing, Elizabeth silently directed all six of us to stand, evenly spaced, just inside the circle. We followed her directions just as silently.

Elizabeth looked at each of us, one by one. Then she said firmly, "Now that we are all here, I want to explain the purpose of this meeting. I have a picture of one of the girls. Now I need a picture of the other one.

One of the unfamiliar guys reached into his pocket, pulled out a photo of a cute young brunette, and handed it to her. She set it on the altar.

"Tonight, I am going to bring a helper from the unseen world to assist us with our great work. After tonight, these two women will be under our control. They will know nothing of our purposes. I consecrate this circle for the work we are going to do this very night."

Elizabeth picked up the wand from the table and pointed it high in the air.

"I conjure thee, spirit of Baphomet. With the power from the Supreme Majesty, I strongly command thee to appear."

She slowly drew an invisible pentagram in the air in front of her.

"I do invoke, conjure, and command thee to appear quickly and show thyself in this circle. I command thee to appear!"

Then she threw her arms out in front of her, breathing heavily. "Ba—pho—met! Ba—pho—met! Ba—pho—met!"

She said the name slowly and forcefully, closing and opening her eyes. "I humbly invoke and beseech you, that you may condescend to come down and appear here before the circle. I order you through the virtue of the one whose name is marked as Baphomet."

She set the wand back on the altar and picked up the dagger. Holding it in her right hand, she turned her body to the left. She said, "Thou art," and touched the dagger to her forehead. Then she touched it to her chest and said, "The kingdom." Touching it to her right shoulder, she said, "The power," and, touching her left shoulder, "And the glory." She clasped her hands and said, "Forever." Then, pointing the dagger upward, she whispered, "Amen." She returned the dagger to the altar.

I thought I saw the outline of a dark shadow appear in the smoke of the incense. Was it real, or was it my terrified imagination?

Next, Elizabeth poured a dark liquid from the bottle on the table into the chalice. She silently passed it to Kenny and motioned for him to take a drink and pass it around. He sipped from it and passed it to me. I smelled the sweet aroma of rum. I took a taste and passed it to Vince. He took a swig and passed it along to the next guy. Eventually it made its way back to the table.

Then Elizabeth took two picture frames out from beneath the altar and set them in front of her. She took the frames apart, then carefully placed the picture of Jackie in one frame and the picture of the second girl inside the other.

Elizabeth placed dried red flowers behind the snapshots and spoke. "The women in these pictures are under our power. I will them to forget. They won't remember any of this. They won't remember a thing."

She waved her arms dramatically over the pictures, picked up the chalice, and sprinkled drops of the remaining liquid on the back of each picture. Then she put the frames back together and wrapped each framed picture in a separate black cloth. When she was done, she set the wrapped-up frames on the floor in front of the altar.

Again, she reached under the table. This time she brought out a small hammer. She knelt in front of the folded cloths and, with a flourish, brought the hammer down gently on the first frame, just hard enough to crack the glass. Then she did the same with the second frame.

She opened the cloths gingerly and announced, "The women in each of these pictures will be under our power. Each is bound by the spirits to do whatever I will her to do."

When the first cloth was removed, I saw the image of Jackie appear, fractured. In that moment I understood that Jackie's life was no longer her own. In the next, with a shiver, I realized that the same was true for me, and Vince, and Kenny.

Satisfied with her spells, Elizabeth picked up her wand and drew another pentagram in the air, but this time in the opposite direction. Then she set the wand on the altar and crossed her arms over her chest.

"Around me shines the pentagram; within me flames the five-rayed star." She threw her arms down to her sides. "I bind the spirit of Baphomet. Do as I say and cause me no harm." She raised her arms once more. "Spirit of Baphomet, I do here license thee to depart. Depart, I say, and be thou very ready to come again at my call. Withdraw now peaceably and quietly, and the peace of the spirits be ever continued, between thee and me."

She fixed her gaze on the six of us clustered inside the circle. "Repeat after me" she said firmly. "Amen."

"Amen," we all intoned.

Elizabeth turned the lights back on and then blew out the black candles. She looked at us and gave us a grim, tight smile.

I looked around the circle. I could clearly see Kenny, Vince, and the other three guys, all looking pale and shaken.

"It is complete," Elizabeth said. "You may go."

She opened the door. Silently, the six of us slithered out.

Kenny and I silently followed Vince back to his room. When we got inside, we all seemed to exhale at once.

"What the hell was *that*?" Vince said finally.

"You work for that crazy bitch," I said. "You tell me. Or are you saying that this came out of nowhere for you, too?"

"*Completely* out of nowhere," Vince said, sitting down heavily on the bed. "Until tonight, that woman has been all business, all the time. I've never seen her spill her coffee or tell a joke."

Kenny said, "I have *never* been so creeped out."

Then they both turned to me, "Donnie," Vince said, "What's your take on what happened?"

For a few seconds I just stood there. Then, finally, some words came out of my mouth. "I have no idea. But I sure as hell hope it works."

15

Tuesday, January 28, 1975
Billboard Hot 100 Hit Song of the Week:
"Please, Mr. Postman" by The Carpenter

I t was about three weeks later, just after 8:00 on a Tuesday night. I had just smoked some hash and pigged out on Chinese takeout when the phone rang. I picked up the receiver eagerly. I figured it was Carol.

"Well, hello," I said in my deepest, sexiest voice.

"Hi, Donnie. It's Elizabeth Corley."

"Hi, Elizabeth." I checked the clock and did a mental calculation. It was past 11:00 in New York. "It's awfully late out east. What's going on?"

"There's someone I want you to meet tomorrow for breakfast. She's helping me with a special project, and I need you to be involved."

"I've already got a breakfast meeting scheduled at the station with Earl."

"It's cancelled," Elizabeth said firmly.

"What? No, it isn't." I took a deep breath. "With all due respect, I work for Earl. I can't just bail on him."

"Listen to me, Donnie," Elizabeth said coldly. "You don't have a choice. I'll deal with Earl." She paused. "You'll be having breakfast at 10:00 with a chick named Ellen. She's flying in from San Francisco early tomorrow. After your breakfast, take her to the station to meet Jackie. You'll tell Jackie she's a promo agent with Groovy Records."

"And then?"

"She's going to invite Jackie to a music industry party in Palm Springs."

"I see. And what am I supposed to do?"

"You're going to make sure Jackie goes to Palm Springs. And you're going to be there, too, to make sure everything goes smoothly."

"But the station..."

Elizabeth laughed dismissively, cutting me off. "Donnie, when you own your own station, you can call the shots. Until then, don't be a prick. Get a pen. You'll need to take notes."

I swallowed hard. "Where should I meet this woman?"

"At the restaurant in the downtown Beach City Inn. I've shown her your picture, so she knows what you look like. She'll be waiting for you. She'll fill you in on all the details and follow you to the station to set everything up. Afterward, she'll say she has more promo calls to make and split."

"What does she look like, this Ellen chick?"

"She's in her mid-twenties. She's got shoulder-length black hair and bangs. She looks like Cher's sister. She'll be wearing a black blouse and jeans. Got all that?"

"Got it."

"Good. And Donnie – no more 'but the station' or 'I already have a meeting' shit. You've seen my daggers. Maybe you saw Baphomet. So, some advice: don't screw with me." And then the line went dead.

The next morning, I did exactly as I was told. I went to the Beach City Inn, parked the Camaro, and found Ellen without any trouble. She was the only customer in the restaurant in jeans. Everyone else was in business attire.

"Hi, I'm Donnie." I extended my hand and smiled. "You must be Ellen."

She didn't smile or get up or move her arm. "Sit down."

I sat.

Ellen looked like any mid-twenties chick in the record business. She wasn't much older than Jackie. I wondered how she got involved with Elizabeth.

She got straight to the point. "When we go to the station after we eat, I'm going to do the usual promo agent shit. I've got a big bag of giveaways in my car. At some point, I'll start chatting with Jackie. Eventually I'll invite her to an industry party in Palm Springs on Saturday, February 15th. I'm going to talk her into driving there and back with me. If she balks or says no, your job is to work on her later, and convince her to go with me. Got that?"

"Sure," I said.

"Have you done this before?" she asked me.

"Maybe."

She grunted. "Listen, this is what's gonna happen. Early on the 15th, I'll fly into town, rent a car, and pick her up. We'll probably get to Palm Springs around 4:00 p.m. and check into the Village Inn motel. You'll get a room at the same motel and wait for my call. Elizabeth will be in from New York with some special guests, but they'll be staying somewhere else. At a certain point, she'll take over. Around eight-thirty I'll call your room, and then you'll do whatever I say. Got it?"

"Yes." What else could I say?

"Now, remember, I'm the promo girl from Groovy Records. That's how you'll introduce me at the station."

"Okay," I said. "What kind of promo items did you bring to give away?"

She looked at me like my very existence bored her. "Donnie, you know how important this is, don't you?"

"I guess I don't."

"A couple of guys are paying a lot of money for this party. *A lot*. They're foreigners. Rich guys. Super-rich."

"You mean they're not the guys I met in Vegas?"

Ellen snorted. "Those assholes? They're nothing next to these guys. We're talking about ancient wealth and royal blood. They get to go first. The Vegas guys will get sloppy seconds."

"Wait," I said. "They sold Jackie to four different guys, all in one night?"

Ellen made a disgusted face. "Ooh, you're right. Two is fine, but four is wrong. What difference does it make? She won't remember a thing."

Unexpectedly, she touched my hand. "Now, after all four men are finished with Jackie, I'll dress her, get her into the car, drive her home, and put her to bed. I'll have a dosed soda ready, so if she wakes up at any point, I'll give it to her and send her back to dreamland. When she wakes up in the morning with a splitting headache, all she'll remember is that she went to a party with me and got wasted."

I took a long breath. "Ellen," I said. "I have to know. What's so damn special about Jackie?"

"That's not my business. And not yours either."

I sighed. "Okay," I said. "Listen, this is supposed to be a breakfast meeting, and I'm hungry as hell. I'm going to order food. Do you want something?"

She gave me that bored-to-tears look again. "Maybe."

Ellen followed me in her rental car. We got to the station a little before noon; Charlie Greene was in the middle of his mid-morning shift.

After I parked the Camaro, we went straight back to my office, and I closed the door. Ellen put her tote bag on my desk and started pulling out the swag. It was the usual stuff, mostly records and T-shirts.

"Ellen," I said. "If you want to get in good with Jackie, tell her you're a fan of Todd Rundgren. Say you saw his band Utopia at the Winterland last year."

"Good. I'll tell her that. Anything else?"

"You could tell her you like the Grateful Dead. She likes them, too."

"Okay." She took a deep breath. "All right, it's show time; let's go. Put on your game face."

I opened the door, and Ellen and I walked out into the music office. Patrick wasn't around; Jackie was on the phone. Ellen and I stood silently for a minute until she hung up.

"Jackie," I said softly.

"Oh," she said, looking up. "Hi, Donnie."

"There's someone I want you to meet. This is Ellen from Groovy Records. She's from the regional office in San Francisco and she came down today to visit some local stations."

Ellen suddenly put on a big glowing smile and stuck out her hand. "It's a real pleasure to meet you, Jackie."

"Same here."

"I brought you some new releases and a couple of t-shirts." She handed the goodies to Jackie. "What do you think of our label? We've got some of the biggest names in rock 'n roll."

Jackie looked at the albums, held up the t-shirts, and smiled. "Thanks, Ellen. Groovy Records has some excellent talent, especially for the urban market. As soon as a song by one of your artists reaches the top 25, we'll be the first to add. Won't we, Donnie?"

I had to stifle a laugh. That was the verbatim script I'd taught Jackie to say to every promo person from every label.

"Absolutely," I said. "Groovy Records has always been a friend to the Harkins radio chain."

Time to go for it.

"Jackie, Ellen is a huge fan of Todd Rundgren's Utopia. Aren't you, Ellen?"

"Yeah, I saw them last year at the Winterland in San Francisco."

"Cool," Jackie replied. "Todd Rundgren's my favorite."

"He's a good producer, too," said Ellen. "He's produced a lot of hits. I heard you like the Grateful Dead, too."

Jackie smiled. "I'm trying to convince Donnie to play 'Truckin'.'" She turned to me and winked.

"Maybe I'll play it late at night," I said. "We'll see."

Ellen took her cue. "Jackie, Donnie has been singing your praises to me. Groovy Records is having a party in Palm Springs in a couple of weeks. There's gonna be a lot of cool people there who could help you with your career. Would you like to go? Donnie just gave me his approval."

"I saw something about that in *Billboard*. But I thought it was only for music directors. Is Patrick invited?"

Ellen looked at me.

"Of course, Groovy Records invited him," I said. "But Patrick's working on air that night. So, I decided that you could go in his place."

Now Jackie looked at me. I felt pinned between two female gazes.

I said," I'd like you to go and represent our station. You'll meet some important industry people, and it will be good for your career in radio."

Jackie nodded then looked back at Ellen who put on a huge smile. "You'll have a blast, and of course Groovy Records pays for everything. I can pick you up and we'll drive there and back together. Have you ever been to Palm Springs?"

"No, I haven't," Jackie answered. "Will we stay at a hotel with a swimming pool?"

Ellen laughed. "Honey, every hotel in Palm Springs has a swimming pool."

"Well... okay." Jackie didn't seem sure. She looked at me again.

"Go for it," I said. "You have my blessing."

Ellen said, "The party is Saturday, February 15. I'll pick you up at noon. Pack your prettiest dress... and a bathing suit."

It was that easy. By the time Ellen left the building, Jackie was looking at the Groovy Records artist list and asking me if I thought any of them would be at the party.

An hour later, Jackie came into my office, with a confused look on her face.

"Donnie, I'm having second thoughts. I want to ask you about that party in Palm Springs. It sounds a little fishy."

I looked up from the stack of carts on my desk. "Of course it's fishy," I said. "It's a way to try to entice our station to play more Groovy Records artists."

"I don't think I'm ready to represent the station. I just got promoted a few weeks ago."

I laughed. "Jackie, don't put yourself down. We have big things planned for you at Harkins Media."

Her eyes widened. "Really?"

"Sure. You've got to learn all about the business, and this is a great way for you to make contacts."

"I don't know. Ellen seems so... pushy."

"That's her job, Jackie. You're being buttered up, big time. The promo people aren't fools. Ellen knows that someday you might be a music director, or even work in the national office. When that happens, she wants to have been your friend for years."

Jackie frowned. "So, I should go?"

"Hell, yeah. You'll probably have a blast, and it will be good for your career. Just so you understand what Ellen's doing. She'll stop being your good friend the day she leaves the industry—or the day you do."

"Okay, Donnie, you convinced me. I'll go."

I watched Jackie turn around to walk back to her office. I knew the night of February 15th would be something I'd remember for a long, long time.

16

Saturday, February 15, 1975
Billboard Hot 100 Hit Song of the Week:
"You're No Good" by Linda Ronstadt

The phone rang in my Palm Springs motel room. It was Ellen. "We're here now, Donnie. I'm at the front desk, checking in. We're in room 118."

"Where is she now?" I asked.

"She's in the car, waiting," Ellen said. "I'll get her settled. You can tell the clients that we'll be at the swimming pool in about half an hour."

"They're already waiting at the pool. I'm on the second floor. I can see them from here. They saw her picture; I'm sure they'll be looking for her."

"Good. I'll call you around eight-thirty. See you then."

"I'll be here."

I looked out my window. From my vantage point, I could see two of the men I'd met in Vegas sitting at the pool. One was fat and hairy; the other, skinny and pale. Covered by towels and eyes hidden by Ray-Bans, they were holding drinks. The skinny guy was chain-smoking.

I watched with disgust and dread as Jackie and Ellen arrived at the pool about 40 minutes later. The two men surreptitiously ogled them as they swam and sunbathed. I even saw the skinny guy cover his hard-on with a towel.

This was all part of the plan. Elizabeth wanted to show off the goods to the customers and get them excited. It also gave Ellen and me chance to observe these guys to see if they were going to be a problem. After watching them for an hour. I was all but certain that they were just two horndogs with money.

Afternoon turned into evening, but I was too keyed up to eat the take-out I'd bought. I chain-smoked, drank soda, and tried to watch TV, but I couldn't concentrate.

The plan was for Ellen and Jackie to get all dolled up for the Groovy Records party. But Jackie would never leave their motel room.

While Jackie got ready, Ellen would go out to get burgers and sodas for the two of them, and return with Jackie's soda spiked. By 8:00 p.m. Jackie would be out cold. At least I didn't have to be the one to administer the knock-out drugs.

I thought about how naïve and trusting Jackie was. She had no idea how fresh and appealing she was to these older guys.

Finally, around 8:15, the phone rang. I picked up the receiver. "Hello?"

"Donnie, it's Ellen."

"Where are you?"

"I'm in the room."

"How's Jackie?"

"Unconscious. I spiked her soda. Game on. Elizabeth is on her way over. I called our second-string customers and told them I would come and get them when it was their turn. You can come to our room now."

"She's going to be okay, right? There's no chance you've put her in a permanent coma?"

106

Ellen snorted. "Donnie, relax. I've done this dozens of times with lots of girls. Eventually so will you."

I stubbed out my cig and crept down the motel stairs to the floor below. I opened the unlocked door to room 118 and tiptoed in. When my eyes adjusted to the dark, I almost fell over.

Jackie was out cold on one of the beds, which had been moved into the middle of the room. She was dressed in a sheer white gown with little flowers on the hem. She looked like a sweet, innocent, sleeping girl from a fairy tale.

I looked up from her still body. The room was filled with people. It took me a while to figure out who was who.

Elizabeth stood next to the bed. She had on the same long, flowing robe she'd worn at the Capri Island Hotel. Our eyes met. She put one finger to her lips, then pointed to where I should stand.

Next to the bed, two men sat in chairs, their backs very straight. They were staring at Jackie. One was old, the other roughly my age. Both wore tailored, elegant-looking clothes.

The older man looked like he was in his seventies. He was tall and thin, with high cheekbones, close-cropped white hair, a large forehead, and a long, straight nose. His blue eyes were framed with gold wire-rimmed glasses.

The younger man had a similar build and features. He resembled the older man; maybe he was his grandson. His black hair was buzzed short, and his chest and arms were muscular, like those of a military man.

Behind them, Ellen stood silently, looking like a maid awaiting instructions. Her gaze was cast down. Like Elizabeth, she wore a black robe.

Elizabeth had created a small altar on a nightstand behind the bed. The altar was covered with a square of red cloth, and there was incense and a pair of black candles burning in the center. A wand, a dagger, a chalice, some cloth, and a carefully rolled-up long red sash were all positioned on the altar. In the center was her magical book, the same one she'd had at the Capri Island Hotel. This time I was close enough to read the faded scarlet imprint on the worn black cover. It said, *The Lesser Key of Solomon.*

Elizabeth had covered the lampshades with red squares of cloth, giving the room an eerie cast. A rope shaped into a circle surrounded the bed. Inside the circle was another rope fashioned into a triangle. Symbols were drawn in red chalk on the wall behind the bed. One was an eye inside a triangle; another was an upside-down cross; and a third was the number 237.

Everyone in the room was still and silent—except for the two seated men, who whispered to each other in a language I couldn't make out.

Ellen handed Elizabeth the wand from the table. She pointed it high in the air and slowly drew an invisible pentagram. Then she threw her arms out in front of herself, breathing heavily.

"I conjure thee, oh spirit of Baphomet, with the power armed from the supreme majesty, I strongly command thee to appear. Ba—pho—met! Ba—pho—met! Ba—pho—met! I humbly invoke and beseech you, that you may condescend to come down and appear inside the circle. I order you through the virtue of the one whose name is marked as Baphomet. Appear quickly and show thyself in this circle!"

She handed the wand to Ellen, who returned it to the table, picked up the dagger, and passed it to her. Holding it in her right hand, Elizabeth said, "Thou art" and touched the dagger to her forehead. She touched her chest with the dagger and said, "The kingdom." Touching her right shoulder, she said, "The power," and, touching her left shoulder, "And the glory." She clasped her hands together and said, "Forever"—then pointed the dagger upward. "Amen." Then she returned the dagger to its position on the altar.

After a pause, Elizabeth silently pointed at the older man. "It is now time to inspect the girl," she said.

He stood up and stepped toward Jackie.

He bent over her and pulled her gown up to her stomach. Then parted her legs with his bony fingers and looked closely at her pussy. He stood there a few moments, peering down. Then he looked toward Elizabeth, who handed him a red cloth. Covering his fingers, he pried open her honeypot, looking for something only he knew about.

"Is she the right girl?" Elizabeth asked. When the man didn't answer, she repeated her question, in what sounded to me like German.

"Ja, ist sie," the old man replied.

"Then we will continue."

The man nodded at his young companion, who stood up and removed his clothing, neatly folding everything and placing it in a pile on the floor. His body was smooth, hairless, and very muscular. His erect, uncircumcised cock stood out in front of him, as if he was going to use it to draw his own pentagrams in the air.

Ellen went into the bathroom and came back with a bowl of water and a small vial. She ceremoniously poured what smelled like fragrant oil from the vial into the bowl and handed it to Elizabeth. Elizabeth dipped her finger in the solution and drew an invisible pentagram on the man's chest. Then he turned around and she drew a second pentagram.

Ellen handed Elizabeth the red sash. Elizabeth unrolled it and started wrapping it around Jackie's right hand.

Then, suddenly, Jackie sat straight up in the bed. Her eyes were wide open.

"Who are you?" she demanded, staring at the older man in front of her. "What are you doing in my room? I'm calling the police."

"My, she's a feisty one," the man said softly in English. He reached out his well-muscled arm and tapped her in the center of her forehead. Jackie closed her eyes and fell back onto the bed.

I almost fell over myself.

Elizabeth didn't miss a beat. She resumed wrapping Jackie's hand with the sash and motioned for the naked young man to kneel above her on the bed. Then she wrapped the other end of the sash a few times around his left hand.

Ellen handed Elizabeth what looked like a pin. She pricked the middle finger of Jackie's left hand, then squeezed it to get out a drop of blood. Elizabeth took the young man's erect cock in her hand and touched it to Jackie's finger, smearing her blood on his cock.

This was his cue. He crouched on top of her, pressed down her shoulders, entered her, and began rocking his pelvis.

While the young man defiled Jackie, Elizabeth loudly recited what sounded to me like an incantation:

> *By air and earth, by water and fire, so the*
> *lamb will be bound, as you desire.*
> *By three and nine, her power I bind, by moon*
> *and sun, your will be done.*
> *Cord go around, force be bound, light re-*
> *vealed, now is sealed.*

The young man ejaculated with a grunt. Then, slowly, he pulled out and rolled to the side, onto his back, his hands and Jackie's still connected by the red sash.

Elizabeth unwound it and handed it to Ellen, who replaced it on the altar. Then Ellen handed her a roll of gauze from the floor next to the bed.

The young man carefully climbed off the bed and knelt next to it holding his sash-covered hand in front of his face. Elizabeth wrapped the gauze around the young man's naked body, from his chest to the top of his thighs. Then she unwrapped and removed the sash. Still wearing the gauze, he stood up and got dressed.

Elizabeth walked back to the altar. The black candles flickered, and the incense had almost burned down. Again, she recited what sounded like an incantation:

> *Solar flare, lunar mist. I call on thee this day.*
> *Bring forth your light, strength, and power,*
> *so cast this spell I may.*
> *I bind thee to Baphomet, the Lord of Darkness.*

She took the dagger off of the altar, pointed it to the four directions, and whispered: "O thou spirit, because thou hast diligently answered my demands and hast been ready and willing to come at my call, I license thee to depart unto the proper place without causing harm to man or beast. Depart I say, I charge thee to withdraw peaceably and quietly, and the peace of God be always continued between thee and me. Amen."

She picked up the chalice and poured a few drops on the altar. Then she took a drink and passed it to Ellen, who did the same.

As she put it down, she said softly, "It is done."

She blew out the two black candles, then took the sash and used it to wipe the writing off the wall. Then she walked over to Jackie on the bed and wiped her down with it.

Very slowly and carefully, she removed Jackie's nightgown and covered her with the sheet. Then she bent over and hissed into Jackie's left ear, "You won't remember any of this. You won't remember a thing."

By now the room was filled with a mixture of odors: the sweet smell of the incense, the acrid odor of the extinguished candles, and the pungent sweat and semen of the young foreign man.

We watched in the dim light as Elizabeth gathered all the items she had used for the ritual and put them in a large satchel. Both she and Ellen removed their robes, revealing their regular clothes underneath. They folded the robes carefully and put those in the satchel too.

Elizabeth looked at each of us in turn, her face a mask of authority. She said softly, "It is done." She pointed to the two foreign men. "You will leave now. We will accompany you."

Silently and obediently, they stood.

Elizabeth looked at Ellen and me. "Bring in the others." Then she and the foreign men filed out the door.

I looked around the room. There was no trace of any of the witchy stuff—just a drugged girl on a bed, ready for two sweaty, horny guys with money.

"I'll get the dudes," whispered Ellen. "You stay here." She tiptoed out of the room.

I heard some noise outside. I was shaking with terror as I crept over to the window and peered out from between the curtains.

It was only the night manager. No doubt he was well rewarded for turning a blind eye toward all kinds of goings-on at his motel. I let the curtains fall closed, then sat on the couch and waited.

After a minute, there was a light knock on the door. A moment later it opened, and Ellen entered with our two horndog clients.

We all looked at Jackie in the dim light, covered by the thin white sheet. She seemed so serene, like Sleeping Beauty waiting for her prince.

"Ain't that a sight," said the skinny one.

"Yeah. It's some good lookin" cooter," agreed the big guy.

They both stood there for a second, deciding what to do next.

"We need pictures, Donnie," the skinny guy said. "Will you take them?"

I hadn't even noticed he was holding a Polaroid camera. He handed it to me. "The film is in there; just take the pictures, okay? We need proof."

The last thing I wanted to do was take pictures.

Ellen sensed my hesitation. "Do as you're told, Donnie," she said sharply. She stepped back into the corner of the room, her gaze hard on me.

I took a long breath and said to the guys, "Go ahead, have your fun, men. I'll take the shots."

"Make sure our faces are in the pictures," said the skinny one. "We need proof."

"Okay," I answered.

The skinny dude went first. He unbuckled his pants and they dropped to the floor. I stifled a laugh as I looked at his chicken legs sticking out of his striped boxers. He peeled off the rest of his clothes, threw them on the floor, and pushed them into a pile.

He climbed onto the edge of the bed on his knees and pulled the sheet off Jackie. Then he opened her legs with his hands and straddled her body, touching it softly at first, then getting rough. He pulled on her breasts and pinched her nipples. Yet he didn't actually enter her. He was just squeezing his cock with his right hand and touching her with his left. It seemed like he wasn't sure what he was doing. Or maybe he was trying to wake her up.

"Take it easy, buddy," I said. What would Jackie think—or do—if she woke up with bruises and scratches?

"Shut up and do your job," the skinny dude snapped. "I won't hurt her." He eased up on her. "Take those pictures, man."

"Okay." I leaned forward and took a shot, terrified that the flash would wake Jackie up. The flashbulb flooded the room with light—but, thankfully, Jackie didn't move or flutter her eyes. I removed the photo from the camera.

The skinny horndog kept working his cock with one hand. Now he was fingering her pussy with the other.

"Take a picture, take it now!" he suddenly shouted. I leaned closer and snapped the shutter. For an instant, the flashbulb bathed the room in light—just as he gasped and sprayed jizz all over Jackie's stomach.

He moaned briefly, then turned to me. "Did you get the shot?"

I nodded. I removed the photo from the Polaroid and handed it to him while he got dressed. I could smell the stink of cigarettes and sperm on his hand.

Meanwhile, the big guy had stripped down, but his cock was only half erect. He stood still, stroking it hard with his right hand. Yet it remained soft. That's what happens when you get old and fat. I watched him climb onto the bed next to Jackie's face, and roughly turn her head toward his cock.

"Careful with the merchandise," Ellen said sternly from the corner of the room.

"Okay," he grunted. Then he pulled her face close to his cock with his left hand and began furiously jerking himself off with the other. He grunted and moaned softly for a few seconds. "I need a picture! Take it now!" A moment later, he ejaculated all over her cheek. I moved in for a shot of his cock resting on Jackie's cheek, with the jizz dripping down her face, and his own grinning face in the background.

The fat man sighed deeply. Then he got off the bed and got dressed. I handed him his photo. "Here you go, dude." Then, wordlessly I handed the skinny horndog his camera.

Ellen hissed from the corner, "Donnie, get me a washcloth. *Now.*"

I jumped at her shrill command. I went into the bathroom, wet a washcloth, and brought it to her. She took it and began to clean up Jackie.

Soon, the men were dressed and standing by the door ready to leave.

"Thanks, man," the big guy told me. "With these pictures, we'll go up a level. This is for tonight." He pulled out a wad of cash and handed it to me.

"Thanks." I took the bread without counting it. I opened the door and let them both out.

Neither of them seemed to enjoy what they did to my poor Jackie. To them, it was only a game that rich dudes played—or a way to get ahead in the Organization.

The two men were almost out the door when I heard the skinny one say, "Let's check out of this dump and drive back to LA."

17

Friday, March 7, 1975
Billboard Hot 100 Hit Song of the Week:
"Best of My Love" by The Eagles

By spring, things at Beach City Top 40 were sailing right along. Every week, at least five jocks from smaller markets sent me airchecks, hoping for a shot at the big time. I was starting to plan our spring contests. I had made a bunch of new friends here at the station.

Jackie was working out fine as my secretary, helping me with all sorts of mundane tasks and fielding calls from the promo men. And I always enjoyed hanging out with Patrick Thomas.

The only thing missing in my life was my Carol, and she and Jason would be moving here soon. She finally took my advice and lowered the price on the Houston house. She'd gotten a buyer, and they would close on the deal in June. Then she and Jason would join me in sunny California.

At the end of a work week in early March, Jackie appeared in my office to go through the morning's mail. There was the usual stuff: a *Billboard* magazine, another one of those airchecks, promotion packages for the Eagles' and Linda Ronstadt's new songs, and the latest *Music Digest*; noth-

117

ing out of the ordinary. Then Jackie picked up a manila envelope marked with a seal from President Gerald Ford.

"What's this?" Jackie asked.

We didn't get mailings from the White House every day. "I dunno. Open it."

She did. It contained a letter and a little red pin, about an inch in diameter, with the word "WIN" printed on it in white capital letters.

Jackie looked over the letter from the President. She said, "The button stands for Whip Inflation Now. President Ford wants all media outlets to announce and support the campaign. He's asking us to broadcast tips for saving energy and fighting inflation."

I shrugged. "We can do that. The station has to provide public service announcements anyway. Listen, why don't you put that college degree to work and write up a list of tips? I'll have the jocks announce them on the air between songs."

"Sure. I'll do that this afternoon. Can I keep the button?"

I shrugged again. "Okay." Chicks always like to keep weird things.

After she left, I sat at my desk thinking about what a sweet kid Jackie was—and how, just a few weeks ago, I had made a couple of grand by helping a bunch of sleazeballs get their rocks off with her drugged, comatose body.

18

Thursday, March 20, 1975
Billboard Hot 100 Hit Song of the Week:
"Black Water" by The Doobie Brothers

It was a few minutes after 6:00. Rockin' Rex had just signed off and Patrick Thomas had signed on. There was a timid knock on my door.

"Who's there?"

"It's me, Donnie." Jackie opened the door a crack and tentatively stepped inside. "Can I come in?"

"Sure. What's up? You're here late. I thought you already took off."

Jackie shut the door behind her and took a seat across from me on my sofa.

"There's something that's really bothering me that I want to talk to you about. Something I promised not to say."

I looked at her red-rimmed eyes. "Let me guess. You've you been smoking pot with Patrick."

She blushed. "That's not the problem."

"Does this have anything to do with Patrick? Are you two getting along okay?"

"Patrick is groovy. This isn't about Patrick."

"Don't make me play guessing games. Spit it out, Jackie."

119

"It's about Kenny," she said softly.

"What about Kenny?"

"You know, um, he's one of my boyfriends, sort of."

"Okay."

"He tells me stuff."

"What kind of stuff?"

"Um... he told me something that got me really upset."

I took a long breath. "Do you mind if I have a smoke, Jackie?"

"I don't mind."

I pulled a cig out of the pack in my jeans, lit up, and took a long drag. I hoped to God that Kenny hadn't snitched to Jackie.

"Jackie, what is it that's bothering you so much?"

"It's about Matt West."

"Matt West is a great guy; he's the best morning man I ever worked with. What did Kenny tell you?"

"He told me that Matt West did something to him—that Matt initiated him. That every jock has to do it."

"Do what?"

She took a deep breath. "Kenny said he had to give Matt a blowjob."

I was so relieved that I almost laughed. But I kept a serious look on my face. I said, "Go on."

Jackie looked down at her platform sandals in embarrassment. "I promised I wouldn't tell anyone."

"It's okay, Jackie; you can tell me."

"He said that Matt West was waiting for him after his shift last Sunday. Matt was at the station to record some commercial voice-adds. He was waiting for Kenny in the parking lot when he finished his shift. He asked Kenny if he wanted to go for a ride in his new Oldsmobile Cutlass and smoke some pot. So, Kenny said sure and got in. They drove around the neighborhood, smoking a doobie and listening to the station. But then Matt drove to a deserted area and pulled over in a spot where no one could see them from the road. Then he pulled out his dick and told Kenny he had to suck it, because he was the newest jock and Matt was the oldest jock, and everyone had to do it, as an initiation."

I'd heard rumors about Matt, but nothing definitive. And this blowjob initiation thing was news to me. I said, "Did Kenny do it?"

"He told me he did it and spit it out. Then Matt just zipped back up and drove him back to the station parking lot, like nothing had ever happened."

"Then what?"

"Then Kenny got into his car and drove home."

I sat in silence for a few seconds. What was I going to tell this innocent young girl?

"You know, Jackie," I finally said, "Sometimes guys do crazy things."

She frowned. "Like demand blowjobs from each other?"

"Do you think maybe Kenny made up that story to freak you out?"

"It didn't sound made up to me."

"Just forget about it, Jackie. It doesn't have anything to do with you."

"But Matt West is such a good guy. Why would he do something like that?"

I nodded. "I see you're concerned. I'll talk to Matt—and I won't tell him how I got my information. I'll get it straightened out. Okay?"

"Okay, Donnie."

"Now, I don't want to hear any more. And don't tell anyone else about it. Just forget you ever heard it. I'll see you in the morning."

I stood by my door as she picked up her bag and walked down the hall in those cute bell-bottoms. She turned around for a second when she opened the glass door and waved good-bye. Then she headed out to her old Chevy for her drive back to the beach.

This wasn't the first time I had heard things about Matt West and guys. But, blowjobs or no blowjobs, Matt West was basically a good guy. He knew a little about the crooked contests, and he probably knew about the payola—but he had no knowledge of Jackie or the other girls, or the secret messages, or the Organization.

I shook my head, grabbed another cig, and got back to my scheduling. I guess in radio, even the good guys aren't really very good.

19

Thursday, April 3, 1975
Billboard Hot 100 Hit Song of the Week:
"Lady Marmalade" by LaBell

The office was buzzing with activity. I grabbed my coffee, looked at the piles on my desk, and checked my production schedule for the week. Nothing too crazy or challenging.

I stuck my head into the music office, where Jackie was sitting at her desk, just hanging up the phone. She was wearing a black Led Zeppelin t-shirt, which made her blue eyes and sun-streaked curls stand out. "Jackie, I'll be in Earl Fredrickson's office to talk about the new contest. Hold my calls."

"Okay, I'll take messages."

Earl was seated at his desk as I walked in and took a seat. He gave me a quick smile. "All right, Donnie, what kind of contest have you dreamed up? Did you talk to Ben Bailey for ideas?"

"Yeah, I talk to Ben all the time, but I made this one up myself."

"Okay. Talk to me. But it's got to be as big as The Best Contest."

When Ben was program director of Beach City Top 40 six years ago, he took our station to the top with The

123

Best Contest. Listeners were tempted with daily promos announcing a lengthy list of exciting prizes. The trick was getting the listeners to think the winner would get every single prize.

In the end, all you had to do to win was call a phone number. When the phone number was finally announced, a third of the city's telephone system was jammed for a half hour. Parts of the county along the coast lost phone service for ninety minutes.

In truth, that long list was a list of options, and the grand prize winner got to choose just one of them. If you listened to the DJs' contest patter carefully, you would figure that out. But most people didn't. They fixated on the list of big prizes and thought the winner would get them all.

That was Ben's specialty, creating clever and appealing promos and contests. I could never replicate the excitement of The Best Contest, but I thought this one was going to be pretty good.

I said to Earl, "It's called the See-Through Safe. We'll have a Plexiglas safe made up with an eight-digit combination lock. Inside the safe will be five thousand dollars. We'll display the safe at the Ocean Breeze shopping center, with an armed security guard at all times. Then we'll give the numbers of the combination one at a time on air, one number per week, but not in the right order. People will have to guess the right order and mail in the numbers on postcards. There are 80,000 combinations, so it could take a while before someone mails in the right one."

Earl tilted his head toward me. "And if we get more than one winning postcard?"

"We won't. The first card we receive with the right number wins. If two winners come in on the same day, it's the first one we grab."

Earl sat back in his chair, thinking. "Ocean Breeze is a big account. We can probably get the prize money from them in exchange for commercials. The safe will bring in lots of traffic for them, so you might even be able to get them to pony up to build the safe."

I nodded. "Exactly what I was thinking. How about the cost of the guards?"

"I know a couple of ex-Navy guys who moonlight doing security. The cost shouldn't be that much," I said.

"Easy for you to say. I have to watch every penny." He folded his hands on his desk. "It's a good idea, Donnie. I'll tell you what. Write up a detailed account of all the expenses for this contest. Figure out costs for construction of the safe and the lock, the guards, printing up signs, renting chairs and tables—everything. I want this budgeted down to the last dollar. Then I'll take a look at it and run it by the executives."

"Got it. Will do." I paused and took a deep breath. "Listen, Earl. I have one question."

"Okay."

"Will the contest be clean?"

Earl's eyebrows shot up. "Maybe. I don't know," he said. "Besides, that's not your business." He thought for a moment. "If we do this, I'll want DJ appearances at the shopping center, especially Rockin' Rex and Matt West."

"Sure."

Earl leaned forward in his chair. "Donnie," he said softly. "One more thing. About Jackie. All the customers were happy with the merchandise."

I swallowed hard. I knew what was coming next.

Earl said, "There's going to be a repeat performance soon."

I couldn't help sighing. "Yeah, I know." I thought of Las Vegas.

"And some other new honeypots, too."

"I see."

"You're going to do more than see," Earl said, his voice suddenly cold and menacing. "You're going to be a key player in part of the setup." He gave me a sudden, feral smile. "One of your skills is organizing events. Contests, live broadcasts—and these as well. You're a good team player, Donnie. Do your job well and you can go far." He let that hang there for a couple of seconds.

Then he stood up. "That's all for now," he said firmly. "Close the door on your way out."

20

Saturday May 10, 1975
Billboard Hot 100 Hit Song of the Week:
"He Don't Love You (Like I Love You)" by Tony Orlando and
Dawn

Every year, Beach City Top 40 sponsored an event called The Walk for Pets and People, a walkathon to raise money and awareness for a great charity. The jocks all got involved and there was lots of corporate sponsorship. This gave us community involvement and station promotion, both at once. Earl Fredrickson's wife, Joan, was president of the women's auxiliary of the charity, so her ladies did the paperwork. That was an immense help.

The ten-mile walk started and ended at Beach City Ocean Park Pier. All week the station took pledges from listeners for two of their favorite jocks, Rockin' Rex Rogers and Patrick Thomas, to complete the walk. Listeners could also walk themselves and get pledges from their friends and neighbors.

We had been promoting the hell out of the walk, with public service announcements every hour calling for pledges. The number we gave out was for the hotline run by the charity, which sent me daily updates on pledge amounts. We were going to bring in $25,000 if everyone who pledged paid up.

The event fell on Saturday, May 10, which turned out to be a perfect, sunny day. I told everyone to meet at the tent at the pier by seven in the morning.

I got to the tent early. Volunteers were already registering walkers. There was a huge display from Safeway, with free cans of soda and sample packs of cookies for everyone.

It didn't make sense to set up a remote, so I'd told Rockin' Rex to report live from pay phones along the route. Our tent was wired for electricity, and it had a giant boom box blasting our station. Slowly the place filled up.

Eventually I found Rex in the crowd. He was wearing his signature cowboy hat, jeans, a station T-shirt, and a denim cowboy shirt. He had wisely substituted sneakers for his usual cowboy boots.

"Hey, man!" I said. "Are you ready for the day?"

"Sure, and so are my little buddies," he said, pointing to the fans surrounding him.

Like always, there was a pack of fans crowding around Rex: a bunch of elementary school-aged kids, some teenagers, and a smattering of parents.

He turned to his entourage. "Are we ready to walk?"

"Yeah! Sure thing! You bet!" the kids and parents shouted.

"Good. But before we go, girls and boys, ladies and gentlemen, what's your favorite radio station?"

"Beach... City... Top... 40!" they screamed in unison.

"Okay, let's go!"

The group fell in step behind him. I watched as they all marched along the marked path. I wondered how far most of those little kids would walk before their moms took them back home.

Walking ten miles on a hot California day isn't easy, but I could see that if you didn't count the blisters and sore feet, the event would be a smashing success. I hung out at the tent by the pier for a couple of more hours, chatting up the volunteers and drinking the free soda.

Eventually I headed back to my pad. I kicked back with a brewski and a joint, thankful that I didn't have to walk the ten miles myself. Some people ran it and finished the course quickly, but most walkers took over three hours.

This was one event that didn't have any dirty business, at least as far as I knew. We had a lot of fun on the air and raised money for a great cause. Jackie took pictures and got a finish-line photo of Rockin' Rex and the Beach City mayor for the *Hit Sheet*.

I was glad I didn't have to do a bunch of coke just to forget what happened. The money was raised honestly and, as far as I knew, it would go where it was intended. It was a relief to do something at Beach City Top 40 that I could be proud of.

21

Friday, July 11, 1975
Billboard Hot 100 Hit Song of the Week:
"Love Will Keep Us Together" by The Captain and Tennille

Carol and Jason finally arrived just before the Fourth of July weekend. It was a glorious reunion. Carol was thrilled with the duplex, and the first thing we did was take Jason to the beach. He had never seen the Pacific Ocean.

When her belongings were delivered, Carol set about arranging and sprucing up our place. After a week, at least a dozen trips to the hardware store, and a giant pile of empty boxes in the dumpster, she was happy with the results. We set up a bedroom for Jason that she filled with his clothes and toys. In the rest of the pad she arranged her things, put up pictures and decorations, and made it feel like home. My bachelor days were now clearly and officially over.

Pretty soon after that, Carol started bugging me about work.

"Honey, I'd really like to see the station and meet some of the DJs."

"Sure, we could do that," I said.

"I wanna meet the DJs," echoed Jason.

"Sure, Jason. But wouldn't you rather go to the zoo?"

"Zoo, zoo, zoo!"

I knew where we were going this Sunday.

"Really, Donnie, I'd like to see the station," Carol said.

"Okay, Carol. I can take you both there sometime. But I have a better idea. Why don't we also invite the jocks over here for a little party?"

She thought about it for a minute, then smiled. "Sure. I can make a spaghetti dinner for everybody."

"Great," I said. "I'll take you both for a quick tour of the building after the zoo on Sunday." Sunday afternoon was when I knew that there would be the least activity at the station—and, I hoped, nothing shady going on. Except maybe Matt West getting a blowjob. "And on the Friday after that, let's have everyone over for dinner."

"I like spaghetti!" Jason said. "Can we have ice cream for dessert?"

"You can have as much spaghetti as you want," I told him. "And we'll get some ice cream, too."

I turned to Carol. "You're gonna love the jocks," I told her. "They're a great group of guys."

22

Friday, July 25, 1975
Billboard Hot 100 Hit Song of the Week:
"Listen to What the Man Said" by Wing

Summer was rushing by. An important event was only two weeks away. It was the Radio Programmers' Convention, sponsored by one of the biggest trade journals in the field, *Only the Hits*. It was going to be held at the five-star Gate Bridge Hotel in San Francisco. I'd get to fly up there for the event, where most of the top Harkins Media people would be speaking on the panels. But the most important event of all was the special evening planned for Jackie. My job was to get her there.

I began setting the trap while I was in her office, going over her photo assignment for the next *Hit Sheet*.

"Jackie, how would you like to go to a radio convention in San Francisco? It's sponsored by *Only the Hits*."

She looked up from her green steno pad. "Oh, yeah, I read about that in the trades. Isn't Elizabeth Corley going to be on a panel? It's called Women in Radio, or something like that."

"Yeah, she is. And Ben Bailey and Lou Arnold are doing a panel on their company, WKR Radio Research."

She smiled. "I'd really like to go to those panels."

"Sorry, Jackie, I can't fly you up for the panels on Friday. I need you here that day. But if you'd like to meet Elizabeth and some of the Harkins Media folks, you can drive up Saturday. Harkins Media will pay for your room and meals, and your gas."

She made a slightly pouty face. "I don't know…"

"And there's going to be a real treat on Saturday night—a private concert of your favorite band."

She nearly jumped out of her chair. "Todd Rundgren's Utopia?"

I smiled. "Okay, your second favorite band. The Grateful Dead."

"Really?"

"Yeah, really."

"Wow. Okay, I'm in. I'll have my own hotel room?"

"Actually," I said, "you'll share a room with Elizabeth Corley. She's the one who told me to invite you." I lowered my voice a bit. "Listen, Jackie. I've been saying good things about you to the Harkins people for a while, and they're finally starting to take notice. I think Elizabeth wants to groom and mentor you for bigger things."

Her face broke into a broad grin. "You mean as a DJ?"

"Bigger." I said. "But I can't speak for Harkins Media's plans. I'm only guessing."

"Wow, that sounds amazing!"

"Plus, you'll get to meet radio people from all over the country."

"Okay, I'm in. Thanks, Donnie."

My stomach had clenched into a tight knot. I want to shout at Jackie to run like hell and never come back. Part of me wanted to follow her out that door. But instead, I just changed the subject to next week's programming.

I knew just what a big deal the San Francisco trip actually was. Harkins Media—or maybe The Organization; I couldn't tell the difference anymore—would make more dirty money. And some really creepy guys would leave San Francisco feeling very happy.

23

Saturday, August 2, 1975
Billboard Hot 100 Hit Song of the Week:
"One of These Nights" by The Eagles

On Thursday morning, I flew up to San Francisco and took a cab to the Gate Bridge Hotel. I checked in and met up with Vince.

The convention was quite the scene. The hotel was flooded with jocks, program directors, promo men, and radio and record executives. All sorts of musicians had been invited and I caught a couple of glimpses of some big stars in the lobby and the coffee shop.

Thursday and Friday whizzed by with panels, lunches, dinners, and visits to hospitality suites filled with record company swag, food, and drinks. If you waited until late at night, there was plenty of blow, too.

On Saturday afternoon I met up with Vince and Elizabeth at the hotel coffee shop. We ordered sandwiches and coffee. While we waited for our food, Vince began looking nervous.

"What's with you today?" Elizabeth asked him. "You seem like you just did a double hit of speed."

Vince looked her straight in the eye. "I hate the way Harkins does things sometimes. He has someone else set up all the details, then forces us to execute them, like we're nothing more than worker bees. And then he threatens to punish us if anything goes less than perfectly, even if the plan is badly designed."

Elizabeth looked at Vince with steel in her eyes. "It's the military model. Forced accountability. It gets results." Her gaze softened slightly. "And it will get results with Jackie tonight, just like it has before."

We all fell silent as our waitress delivered our meals.

When she had gone, I stared into my coffee and quietly asked Elizabeth, "How many stations do you think are involved with the Organization?"

She looked at me hard and raised her eyebrows. "Harkins Media stations? All of them."

"No, I mean stations in general."

"About 40 percent," she said. "There's also a major record company involved."

"No shit!" Vince said, suddenly looking even more nervous.

Elizabeth leaned forward. "Okay, boys," she said. "This is how it's going down."

Vince and I both leaned in.

"She knows about the private Grateful Dead concert tonight. You're the one who told her, Donnie, aren't you?"

"Yeah, I used it to convince her to come," I said.

"I'll take her to the concert myself. I don't need you boys," said Elizabeth. "You two stay behind. Besides, Vince has told me more than once how much he hates hippie music."

Vince nodded.

"I'll treat her like a VIP. I'll sit right next to her and when she isn't looking, slip something into her drink. When we get back to the hotel I'll give her a second dose. That's when I'll need your help, Donnie. Since she's staying with me, you'll help me get her into my room so I can get her ready."

She pointed at the two of us. "When Jackie and I get back from the concert, I need you two waiting in the lobby bar. Stay there and watch for us. I don't want Jackie to go astray or disappear with some dude. Run whatever interference you need to."

Suddenly I wanted to cry. But I simply nodded.

"After the concert, there'll be a special event for a group of guys." Elizabeth said.

"Something like Capri Island?" Vince asked.

"Something like that." Elizabeth replied. "It'll be in the Harkins Media suite down the hall from my room, Okay?"

"Yeah," I answered.

"Then, after that, will be the private party in my room. Rich will be there. You two remember him from Vegas, right?"

"Yeah, we remember," I said for both of us. The real reason Jackie was invited.

Then Elizabeth turned her head slowly toward me. She gave me a sudden, huge, gleaming smile.

"You're going to be there for everything, Donnie."

"Me? What for?"

The smile disappeared. "Because I'm telling you to. Because Harkins wants you there. Is that 100% clear?"

My heart clutched "Uh huh."

"All right. One other thing, just so you know."

"Yeah?" I said.

"I brought a movie camera to film the whole evening. It's a special low-luminosity camera that can record in candlelight. I'll set it up after Jackie's knocked out."

I couldn't help myself. "For what?" I asked.

"We call it a control file."

I let out a huge sigh. Vince looked at me, but Elizabeth ignored it.

"All right boys, do you get it?"

"Got it," Vince and I said in unison.

Elizabeth stood up, straightened her jacket, and picked up her purse. "I have a meeting with Nick Mitchell and Henry Harkins in an hour. They're taking the red eye back to New York tonight, and the three of us have a few things to discuss. Go have fun and wait for Jackie. Call me when she gets here and send her up to my room. Any questions?"

"I have one," I said.

Again, she flashed me that enormous smile. "I thought so. But you don't get to ask it, Donnie. Shut up and just do as I say."

We spent the rest of the afternoon wandering around the hospitality suites, picking up free t-shirts, shooting the shit with record promoters, and drinking. Vince was an expert at all three.

Around 5:00 p.m. we made it back to his room. He locked the door and pulled out his stash. We raided the mini bar, smoked a couple of doobies, and waited for the call.

At 6:45 the phone rang. It was Jackie. "Hey, Donnie, I'm here. I parked in the hotel's underground lot."

"Welcome, Jackie," I said, my guts churning. "Go on up to room 516. Elizabeth is waiting for you there. We'll meet you in the lobby at seven-thirty. A bus is going to take everyone to the Grateful Dead concert."

"Cool. See you soon."

I called Elizabeth. "She's on her way."

Elizabeth cleared her throat. "All right, worker bees," she said firmly. "Get ready for showtime."

At seven-thirty, the two of us met Jackie in the lobby. She was standing with Elizabeth in her station T-shirt, bell-bottoms, and sneakers. She carried a white windbreaker and her green bag.

"Jackie, you made it. How was your drive?" I asked.

"It was okay, a lot farther than I thought. Are you going to the concert?" she asked.

"I don't think so." She looked hurt but I assured her, "I'll catch up with you afterward."

Elizabeth jumped in, "Stick with me, Jackie, we're going to have a great time. I'll take care of you."

The bus pulled up and the crowd started piling on. Me and Vince watched Jackie and Elizabeth go up the stairs of the bus. For a second, Jackie turned around to look back at me. Vince elbowed me in the side to signal his approval of her cute little ass.

The show must have ended around eleven-thirty because the bus returned to the Gate Bridge Hotel around midnight. Me and Vince were waiting at the lobby bar when Elizabeth and Jackie returned. When they came through the entrance, we got up to greet them. Elizabeth was holding on to Jackie, whose glassy eyes signaled the pills were working.

"How was the concert?" I asked.

Jackie just stood there smiling but Elizabeth answered, "Great Donnie, just great. Listen," she said. "Can you and Vince wait here a second while we duck into the lady's room? I'll take Jackie with me."

"No problemo," I said, and they both disappeared.

We waited for a long time, until finally Elizabeth emerged from the ladies' room alone, with a frantic look on her face. "I need your help! She passed out."

"What?" I answered.

"I was washing my hands and waiting for Jackie, but she didn't come out of the stall. I banged on the door, and she didn't answer . I didn't know what to do. Finally, I crawled under the stall to unlock the door, and there she was, passed out on the toilet . I need your help!"

This was a side of Elizabeth I hadn't seen before. She was frantic.

"Calm down, Elizabeth," Vince said, "Me and Donnie will take care of it. I'll guard the door and you two go in and get her."

We walked over to the lady's room, and fortunately no one else was around. Elizabeth led me over to a stall and there she was, slumped to the side, passed out on the toilet. Thankfully, dressed. I summoned Vince. We shook her awake and picked her up. Crisis averted.

"Let's get her up to my room," said Elizabeth, and we dragged her over to the elevators to take her upstairs.

I coaxed her on to the elevator, "C'mon Jackie, the party's just starting."

"Donn...eee," she slurred. "It was bitchin...."

"What was, Jackie?"

"The Grateful Dead, I looove them."

"Yeah, yeah, I heard it was a great show," I told her. "C'mon Jackie. Elizabeth needs you, she's right here."

We got to the fifth floor and the three of us maneuvered Jackie into the room. I sat her down on one of the twin beds. Elizabeth felt relieved.

"I'll take over, Donnie," she said, steadying the girl by the arm and handing her a soda with a straw. It contained the second dose. Jackie was going to be out of it for hours.

"Vince," she said, turning toward him, "You can go down the hall to the Harkins Media suite, it's on the other side of the elevators. "Go entertain the guests, tell them me and Donnie will be there in about fifteen minutes."

"Okay," he said, and disappeared.

By now Jackie was deeply asleep on the bed, and the drugs would keep her that way for a long time. I closed the door after Vince and Elizabeth turned off all the lights except in the bathroom.

Elizabeth started undressing her, while I stood to the side and watched.

Once Jackie was naked, Elizabeth covered her with a sheet. Then she went to the closet, took out her satchel, and placed it on a chair.

She pushed a nightstand to the foot of the bed. Then she reached into her satchel and began pulling out supplies. She unfolded a black cloth and draped the it over the nightstand. She set up three candles in a row, two black ones at either end and a red one in the middle. She brought over a small vase with a few flowers from the dresser, and placed sticks of incense in it. Then she carefully put a small bottle, a dagger, and a deck of cards on the nightstand.

Next, Elizabeth took chalk out of her satchel. She knelt and drew a triangle on the carpet underneath the bed. It came to a point on the floor by Jackie's head. She drew a circle around the triangle. Then she paused, stood up, and surveyed her handiwork.

"Elizabeth" I whispered. "What's going to – ."

Without looking at me, she slapped my chest with the back of her hand.

"Shut up. I'm almost done." Then she lifted the card deck, picked out four cards, and placed the rest of the deck on the altar. They were picture cards—tarot cards. In the dim light, I could just barely make out the images. Elizabeth placed one by Jackie's head—the Devil. She placed the Hierophant at

Jackie's feet. On her right side of her sleeping body, the High Priestess. And on her left side, the Magician.

Then Elizabeth picked up the small bottle, shook and opened it, and put a few drops of red liquid on Jackie's forehead. It looked like blood, but I wasn't sure.

Elizabeth moved a chair in front of a tall armoire in the corner of the room. She stepped on it and reached up. I followed her arm with my gaze and saw the movie camera resting on top. Elizabeth turned it on. What had she called it? The control file.

As a final gesture, Elizabeth bent over the bed and whispered in Jackie's ear, "You won't remember any of this. You won't remember a thing." Then she grabbed the satchel and nodded toward me. Together, we left.

We stood in the long, empty hall. I looked at Elizabeth for guidance, but she didn't move and didn't speak.

"Damn," I finally whispered.

She looked at me with disdain. "Keep quiet and watch," she hissed. "And be ready to follow my instructions."

"I don't get it. Why do you need me here at all, Elizabeth?"

She glared at me. "Donnie. Your job is to follow directions. Or is that not yet 100% clear?

I swallowed hard. "It's clear."

"So shut up and follow them. And don't worry. You'll have your own chance to join the fun."

Oh shit. "What if I won't want to join the fun?"

The next thing I knew, her hands were on both sides of my jaw and squeezing hard. Her face was inches from mine. She said calmly, "When I tell you to fly to San Francisco, you fly to San Francisco. When I tell you to screw a girl, you screw the girl." That big, cruel smile appeared again. "I like you, Donnie. In fact, I like you so much that I'm going to do you a favor. I'm not going to break your goddamn jaw."

She removed her hands, still smiling. "Next time it will be your balls. Now follow me." Picking up her satchel, she turned and headed down the hall.

I kept silent until we reached the suite. A few more guys had joined the group . Now there were at least a dozen, plus me. There were radio guys, record company guys, and a couple of musicians. They were milling around, drinking, smoking pot, and talking. Rich was there, too, off in a corner engrossed in a conversation.

I saw Vince near the booze, talking with what looked like a couple of musicians. I made my way over to them.

"Hey Donnie," Vince said. "Is everything ready?"

"Yeah."

Suddenly I thought I recognized the guy on Vince's right. "Aren't you the keyboardist for —"

He cut me off. "Yeah, I'm in the band,"

"We play your records all the time."

He nodded. "Thanks, man."

Vince said, "Our keyboardist friend here is one of our participants this evening. He has a special interest in spells and witchery."

"Do you actually believe any of this?" I asked him. "I mean, the spells and the evil spirits and shit? Or is it all just a way to add to the thrill?"

"Maybe yes, maybe no." He looked at me intently. "There might be something to it. Sometimes I think there definitely is."

"What makes you think that?" I asked.

"Think about it, man. It's got to be the black magic. How else would a shitty band like mine get to be so popular?"

He had a point.

"I did something like this once before, for my band," he said. "We conjured Lucifer himself. He made our wildest dreams come true." His tone was completely earnest. "But the ritual we're doing tonight is different—it's for personal power. We're going to sacrifice the lamb."

My spine tingled. What were they going to do to Jackie now?

Rich, the general manager from Tampa, walked over to me from the other side of the room. "Hey Donnie, remember me from Vegas? What's goin' on?" he said.

"Of course I remember you. Oh, you know, playin' the hits, giving away money." I answered.

A big guy with a bushy beard walked over to join our conversation. He didn't look like an executive, maybe he was a jock.

"Donnie Dixon," I extended my hand. "What brings you here?" I asked him.

"I'm Lucas, I've known Elizabeth a long time. Good to meet you man." We shook hands and he quietly added, under his breath, "I'm a warlock."

"You mean, like the motorcycle gang?" I asked.

He leaned forward and whispered in my ear, "No man, not motorcycles, a coven."

Rich didn't hear what Lucas said. He jumped into the conversation and introduced himself.

Lucas continued, "There's a bunch of us here tonight, man. We're all in the business in one way or another."

"Really?" said Rich.

"Yeah, man, I work for a big company that's into music and movies,"

"I'm impressed," said Rich, "What do you do...?"

I was feeling sick to my stomach. I wanted to run, but all I could do was stand there and listen to Rich and Lucas compare notes. Lucas said he was an A & R man, which is a talent scout for a record company. That is, when he wasn't doing witchcraft.

I excused myself to go to the bathroom to splash cold water on my face but by then Vince was in there with some of the other guys, smoking a joint.

I got them out, closed the door, took some deep breaths and washed up. When I came out, groups of men were still talking, drinking, and smoking, just like any ordinary business meeting. But in a moment Elizabeth would take charge, and things were going to get serious.

"It's time." Elizabeth announced loudly, sounding like an executioner. Everyone stopped talking and looked at Elizabeth.

"We all know why we are here, and I want you to all listen closely and follow my instructions. Please move to the sides of the room, while I make the preparations." The men did what they were told and moved out of her way.

Elizabeth set out her satchel and pulled out the chalk. I watched with curiosity and fear as she marked the floor with a large circle and drew a large triangle in the center of the circle. All eyes were on her as she silently pointed to one of the record guys, who helped her drag a nightstand into the middle of the triangle. Next, she took a red cloth out of the satchel, and covered the nightstand, creating a make-shift altar.

She placed the candles in a row on the altar, just like in the bedroom, with two black candles on the outside and a red one in the middle. Then she carefully arranged the other items: incense, a chalice, a bowl, a dagger, a long wand, and a small book.

When everything was set up, Elizabeth turned to the group and said loudly, "I will now make my final preparations. Wait here," she commanded. Then she picked up her satchel, took it into the bathroom and closed the door.

We all stood in small groups nervously finishing our drinks and making small talk. Vince made his way over to me, obviously high.

"More party games from Elizabeth Corley, she's takes this all so seriously," he laughed.

"You better not get on her bad side," I warned Vince. "I think she's dangerous."

"She won't last in radio, you'll see," he said. "I don't like this, and I don't like her. I'm gonna get her fired. Maybe I'll tell Nick Mitchell's wife about her."

"Shut up, Vince. I just don't want her black magic on me. Besides, it's about to begin," I said.

The bathroom door opened, and Elizabeth emerged, transformed.

Her hair was brushed back, and she had applied blood red lipstick. She wore the long, flowing robe. On her left middle finger was the silver ring with the dark red stone in the middle. On her right hand was a wide ring with symbols etched into the silver.

She strode into the middle of the room and waited until the talking stopped. In an authoritative voice, she announced, "It is almost time to begin. Take your places." She pointed to each of us, one at a time, directing us to stand around her in a circle, about a shoulder's width apart. As I took my place, I looked around. Vince was on my right: Rich was on my left.

Elizabeth had one last, creepy thing in that satchel—a stack of black hoods. She picked them up and handed a bunch to each of the two men standing on either side of her. One was a tall, pony-tailed hippie; the other was a short dude with a Fu Manchu moustache and glasses. Lucas stood next to him.

"Pass out these hoods," she said firmly. They did. When everyone in the room was holding one, she demanded, "Put them on." We did.

Now there were thirteen grown men in hoods standing in a circle, with a witch in the middle.

Elizabeth announced, "It is time to begin."

She lit the candles and incense and turned off all the other lights in the room. She told us, "Stand shoulder to shoulder around the edge of the circle, but do not step inside the triangle of power. I am going to invoke the spirit of the god Pan to help all of you succeed in the music business."

She picked up the dagger and started pointing it in different directions. Then she waved the dagger, making a cross and then a pentagram in the air. She touched the dagger to her forehead, her chest, and her right shoulder. Then she turned in a circle, one direction at a time, and said, "To thee... the Kingdom... the power... the glory... for all the ages... repeat after me, Amen."

We all intoned, as if we were in church, "Amen."

She crossed her arms in front of her. "Before me, Raphael; behind me, Gabriel; on my right, Michael; and on my left, Ariel."

Then she made more signs in the air and said, "Around me are the flames of the Dark Lord. Amen. Say it again with me."

Again, we all chanted, "Amen."

She replaced the dagger on her altar. She picked up the wand and pointed it at Vince, Rich, and me. All the heads in the room swiveled toward us.

She motioned the three of us to walk forward from the circle, up to the triangle on the floor. Then she had us stand in a line facing her. Raising the wand, she began an invocation:

149

"These are the men who will sacrifice the lamb tonight. Now I will bring forth Pan, the god of music, who will give these men the power they seek." For a few seconds she stood silently, her chest heaving. Then she half-shouted, "I conjure thee, oh spirit of Pan. With power armed from the Supreme Majesty, I strongly command thee to appear."

I didn't see anything unusual. But I suddenly sensed that somehow, something was watching us.

"I do invoke, conjure, and command thee, Pan, to appear and show thyself in this circle." Then she put down the wand and opened the small book on the altar.

The black and red candles flickered. The scent of incense barely covered the smell of the joints the men had been smoking. I knew that everyone in the room was out of their mind from drugs, booze, or both.

Reading from the book, Elizabeth chanted,

Come to me, run to me,
Great god Pan! Our great god Pan!
The pipes are playing,
We sing and we stand,
Your lust is our pleasure,
Our great god Pan!
We see you, the horned one,
Half goat and half man,
Take what you want, and
Do what you will!
Your lust is our pleasure,
Our great god Pan! Our great god Pan!

She set down the book and looked slowly around the circle. "Repeat after me and say these words three times: sacrifice the lamb."

We all shouted, "Sacrifice the lamb! Sacrifice the lamb! Sacrifice the lamb!"

Still standing in front of the altar, Elizabeth picked up the chalice and poured some of its contents into the bowl. Then she passed it to the three of us and told us to each take a sip. The liquid was sweet. Once again it was an offering of rum.

After we drank, she passed the chalice around the entire circle of men. Each one took a drink. Then she replaced the chalice on the altar.

Elizabeth continued: "I bind thee, oh Great Spirit of Pan. Give each of these men power in the realm of music. Do as I command, Pan, oh Pan."

We all waited for something to happen—a crack of thunder, or a gust of wind that would blow out the candles. But of course, nothing happened. We all just stood there, still and silent, for about half a minute.

Then Elizabeth slowly nodded. She intoned, "This being done, I do hereby license thee, Pan, to depart to the proper place. Do no harm to man or beast. Depart, I say, being duly exorcised and conjured by the sacred rites of magic. I charge thee to withdraw peaceably and quietly, and the peace of God be continued. Amen."

Instinctively, we all chanted, "Amen."

"Now," Elizabeth commanded, "The sacrifice is about to begin. Remove your hoods. Those who are commanded, go and seek the lamb."

We all removed our hoods, and the circle broke apart. Elizabeth removed her robe, folded it neatly, and put it under the altar. Then she blew out the candles and motioned Vince, Rich, and me to follow her. We left the suite, walked down the hall, and entered Elizabeth's room.

Jackie was still out cold on the bed, covered with the thin white sheet. Elizabeth fished a lighter out of her pocket and lit the candles and incense on the table. I figured there would be more incantations, to go with the candles, incense, and tarot cards on the bed, but Elizabeth simply stood off to the side.

Rich turned to her, his face suddenly twisted in anger. "I thought I got the chick to myself. I paid big money for this."

Elizabeth gave him an enormous smile. "You *do* get her to yourself—for the next ten minutes. Now hurry up and get started. The clock's ticking."

Rich grunted. He walked over to Jackie and pulled off the sheet. For a few seconds he just looked at her lying there, naked and unconscious. Then he slowly undressed, carefully folding his pants and shirt and putting them in a neat pile. He crept onto the bed and pushed off the cards.

Rich toyed with the sleeping girl, just to make sure she wouldn't wake up. He picked up her arm and dropped it. He squeezed her nipples, then rubbed her pussy. Finally, satisfied that she was asleep, he crawled on top of her and started screwing her.

After he did that for a while, he pulled out and crawled up over her body, getting close to her face. Holding the back of her head with his left hand, he pumped his cock into her mouth. This went on for a couple of minutes.

When he got tired of that, he crawled to the side of the bed and turned her over. She moaned slightly but remained unconscious. He pushed her legs apart with his knee, spit on his hands, and moistened his cock. He tried to shove it in her ass, but it kept slipping out.

Rich gave up on that orifice. He pulled her up so her ass was in the air and shoved himself into her pussy one more time. He held onto her hips and pumped her, squeezing her tits before finally spraying his thick load all over her little butt.

I turned away. I'd seen enough. More than enough.

I heard Rich roll off the bed, scuttle to a corner, dress, and leave the room. When I heard the door close, I turned back around.

Elizabeth was pointing to Vince, who was slouching against the far wall with a beer and a cigarette. To my shock, he put down his beer and stubbed out his smoke. He stripped down and clambered onto the bed. He pushed Jackie's legs apart and hovered over her, grinning. Then he grabbed his cock, stroked it a few times until it was erect, and thrust it inside her. I shuddered at the sight of his hairy ass, hoping the red pimples on it were not from some disease.

I looked at Jackie's angelic face, eyes still closed, and watched her body sway as Vince pushed into her. He didn't look at Jackie's face at all. He kept pumping, harder and harder, grunting and moaning, his eyes closed and his face tightly clenched. I almost vomited.

Vince finally let out a long, loud grunt. He pulled his cock out from between her legs and ejaculated on her pubic hair. Then he stroked out the last bit.

He jumped off the bed like it was radioactive and staggered toward me, naked.

My legs were shaking. I sat down in a chair and took several long, deep breaths.

"What a piece," Vince hissed in my ear. "I could do that all day long." I turned away from him and made a shooing gesture with my hand. He returned to his spot in the corner, swilling down the last of his beer, buck naked, without missing a beat.

Elizabeth looked at me. "Now you."

I shook my head.

Elizabeth tightened her jaw and scowled. Slowly and deliberately, she walked to the altar and picked up the dagger. She turned, pointed it at me, and began moving toward me.

"Okay," I told her. "I'll do it."

She lowered the dagger and nodded toward the bed.

I had fantasized about making love to Jackie for such a long time. But I didn't want it to be like this. I wanted it to be real. But what I wanted was not part of what I had to do.

I stripped, threw my clothes in a heap on the floor, and climbed on the bed next to Jackie. She looked so serene lying there in drugged sleep. I lightly caressed the side of her body, tracing the contours of her hips with my fingertips. I brushed over her wet public hair and gently stroked her thighs. My fingers traveled up her body and I circled her nipples, one at a time.

Soon my cock was, engorged and ready. I pressed it inside her. I closed my eyes and went to another place.

Her breasts rose and fell with her breath, and I floated above her. In my imagination, I was alone with her in her bedroom by the beach, and we were sharing the most exquisite kiss. Her arms were wrapped around me, and she whispered in my ear, "I adore you." I brushed loose strands of her hair away from her face and she gently held my shoulders as I entered her. It was everything I wanted, everything I dreamed about, me and this beautiful girl, after all these months, finally together.

I floated like this for a few more moments until I dropped back into my body, which was furiously penetrating her with anger and lust. Over and over, I pounded myself into her, harder and harder, faster and faster until I climaxed in a convulsed rush with an animal-like cry.

As soon as I finished, I opened my eyes, ashamed and embarrassed. I quickly pulled myself out and got off the bed.

After it was over, I felt a strange sense of power and relief. It was a mixture of invincibility, disgust, and fear.

Quickly and quietly, I grabbed my clothes and dressed.

Elizabeth turned on a light. The candles had burned down, and the incense was finished. The tarot cards were somewhere on the floor, and the chalk lines were partly smudged off the carpet.

Elizabeth covered Jackie back up. Then she turned, and with the back of her hand, shooed Vince and me out of the room.

In the morning, Vince and I packed up, checked out, and went to Elizabeth's room. When we got there, Jackie was still asleep. Elizabeth told us that she woke up soon after dawn. Elizabeth gave her some dosed-up orange juice, and she fell quickly back to sleep. Elizabeth assured us that she would sleep the whole way home. Elizabeth had gotten Jackie dressed and packed up her little blue suitcase and that ugly green tapestry hippie bag.

Elizabeth ordered me to drive Jackie and her car back to Beach City, even though I'd have to lie to Carol about getting back late.

When we got back to Beach City, I parked in Jackie's spot at her building. Jackie was only semi-conscious, so I had to drag her and her suitcase to her apartment. The lights and the TV were on, so I had to think fast.

Her roommate let us in. She had been making dinner when I got there and came to the door in an apron. I had never met her before; she was a busty, dark-haired, homely girl. She wanted to know why Jackie was so incapacitated. I quickly made up a story about Jackie accidentally eating three hash brownies and how I had to drive her all the way back myself. I told her it was a great sacrifice because I was supposed to fly home. The way I told the story I made myself look like a hero for taking care of poor Jackie and seeing her home safe. I don't think the chick was convinced.

The two of us walked Jackie into her bedroom, laid her on her bed, took off her sneakers, covered her up, and turned off the lights so she could sleep it off. The room was just like I imagined it: the bed on the floor covered with a red paisley Indian bedspread, a drip-candle wine bottle on the dresser, and band posters on the walls.

I thanked Jackie's roommate profusely, still pretending to be the good guy. As soon as I could, I ran out of there, grabbed my bag, lit up a cig, and walked the two miles back home.

When I finally got home and opened the door, Jason was asleep, and Carol was waiting. I was never so happy to see her in my entire life.

24

Monday, November 17, 1975
Billboard Hot 100 Hit Song of the Week:
"Island Girl" by Elton John

Summer was long over. It was almost Thanksgiving. The last few months had been non-stop work. After the See-Through Safe contest, we sponsored several other contests and publicity events. We put on a free family concert at the end of the summer just for fun, and I let Jackie plan the whole event. We reserved a stage at a city park the weekend before Labor Day and presented two local rock bands. About 500 listeners showed up, and we gave out lots of stickers and swag. It was a great promotion that barely cost the station a thing.

We ran another big contest for the September—October rating sweeps called The Collector Car Contest. We teamed up with an affiliated car dealership to feature their high-octane muscle cars, classic models, a couple of sports cars, and our own station van. We displayed the cars at different shopping centers, and listeners had to fill out a paper "road map" using clues we broadcast on the air. The winner got a new Ford Mustang from one of our biggest advertisers, Gress Motors. Again, it barely cost us anything. Everything was traded for commercials.

But just after Halloween, things at Beach City Top 40 didn't seem quite right. The station sounded great, our ratings were up, and I had done exactly as I was told . I'd put all the bad stuff in the back of my mind, especially when I had to work side by side with Jackie. Something was wrong; I could feel it. Earl was suddenly refusing my requests to plan our contests for the first quarter of 1976.

Nick Mitchell hardly ever called me, but a week before Thanksgiving, he did. He told me that Beach City Top 40 might be changing direction soon, and that I might be leaving for another station in the chain. I thanked him for the advance notice.

The moment after we hung up, I called Vince.

"Vince, Buddy, we need to talk."

"Donnie, I've been expecting your call. Nick called you, didn't he?"

"Yeah. So, tell me straight, what did I do wrong?"

"Nothing. There's just this other guy."

"What guy?"

"He's a program director from New York who's really tight with Henry Harkins," Vince said.

"And?"

"I think they're in a club or something."

"What kind of club?"

"I dunno. It's a men's club."

"The Rotary? The Odd Fellows? The Masons?"

"I'm not sure. It's not a college fraternity or anything like that. It's got some kind of comic book name. The Free Birds, the Seven Rays, the Green Hornets, I'm not sure. Oh, yeah—it's called the Fire Birds. They keep it a secret. Harkins thinks I don't know about it."

"So? What does this have to do with me?"

"It looks like he'll be in and you'll be out—probably after Christmas."

I slapped my hand hard on my desk. "Shit."

Vince paused. Then he said, softly, "Plus, you know how the big boys like to play with people. They're busting your balls. They're moving you because they can."

I sighed. "So that's it? I'm kicked to the curb?"

"No," said Vince. "You're good at what you do, and they know it. They'll find you something else at another station."

"Like what?"

"I'm not sure, but it won't be a demotion. They'll assign you to raise the ratings at another station. Or to do some of the other things you've had experience with. It'll be okay. The worst thing that can happen is you'll have to move."

"Vince," I said. "Carol and Jason just moved here a few months ago. I'm trying to raise a family here."

Vince snorted. "Yeah, that's you—Ward Cleaver. Donnie, if you want stability, become an accountant. Otherwise, you're gonna have to roll with the punches like the rest of us."

25

Monday, January 12, 1976
Billboard Hot 100 Hit Song of the Week:
"Convoy" by C.W. McCall

Moving on in radio is a given—but when it happens, it's always a shock.

On a cool, clear Monday in January, I was called into Earl Fredrickson's office right at 9:00 a.m. When I walked by Jenny, Earl's secretary, she gave me a funny look, so I was ready to hear bad news.

But I wasn't ready for what I saw. Sitting next to Earl was the owner of Harkins Media, Henry Harkins.

"Have a seat, Donnie," Harkins said stonily. Earl said nothing.

I sat.

"I'm sure you know why we called you in today," Harkins said. "I know you've been in touch with Vince."

"You're here to personally congratulate me on the great Arbitron ratings?"

Harkins grimaced and shook his head.

Earl finally spoke. "You know how things change in radio," he said. "And Henry is here today to offer you another opportunity."

"We know you have good numbers," Harkins said. "But it's time to shake things up a bit. We want you at Midwest Music FM as its director of programming."

It figured. I was being moved from Beach City to the snowbound middle of nowhere. Radio was an endless game of musical chairs. And this time I was the loser.

Harkins said, "We need you to boost the ratings there. They're good, but we think you can make them better. The station has some stiff competition, but we have faith that you can do it. We also need you to bring in more advertising dollars." He paused. "And we need you for some other, less radio-oriented tasks."

"You want me to find more girls for your people to pimp." There, I'd said it.

Earl said, "This isn't a demotion, Donnie. Henry will even give you a salary bump. Two grand more per year."

"My wife and stepson just moved here to be with me six months ago. Doesn't that matter to you?"

Harkins didn't even blink. "No, it doesn't matter to me, Donnie. And it never will. You can do what I say, or you can resign. You're my employee. You're expected at Midwest Music next week."

I took a deep, slow, breath. "I want a 15 percent salary increase and all my moving expenses. Not just two grand."

Harkins smiled. "No. Ten percent and moving expenses."

"And I need a full two weeks to get my things in order and get there."

"Done." Harkins looked at his watch, then back at me with an obvious lack of interest. "Donnie, you're gonna love Midwest Music. They're one of our highest-rated FM stations, and they're huge in the market, just beneath the news station."

"Got it. Can I bring any of my DJs?"

"We'll see about the jocks—you might be able to bring one or two—but we'll need that chick Jackie there. Make sure she comes with you."

That stopped me cold. "And how am I supposed to arrange that?" I knew there was anger in my voice, but I didn't care.

Harkins raised his eyebrows. "Offer her a full-time job as your music director. She'll follow you to Antarctica for that."

I felt like I was going to faint. I nodded and started to get up to leave.

"Oh, Donnie," Harkins said. "One more thing."

"Yes?"

Harkins stood up and brushed something invisible from the arm of his suit jacket. "Never, *ever* challenge me again."

I froze. But Harkins had already turned away and was reaching for an ashtray on Earl's desk.

"Thank you, Donnie, for everything you did for Beach City Top 40," Earl said, offering his hand.

I almost threw up, but I put out my hand to shake his. "I enjoyed collaborating with you, Mr. Fredrickson."

Ten minutes later, I was standing outside in the parking lot, blinking in the morning sun, holding a cardboard box full of my personal stuff.

Now I had to go home and tell Carol.

Part Two

Part Two

26

Monday, February 2, 1976
Billboard Hot 100 Hit Song of the Week:
"Love Rollercoaster" by The Ohio Players

When Harkins Media purchased Midwest Music FM in 1971, it immediately changed the format from easy listening to Top 40 and hit album tracks. It upgraded the station's power from 50,000 to 100,000 watts and brought in a program director from another Harkins station to steal listeners from the local powerhouse AM station. It established a high-energy sound tweaked by Nick Mitchell and Elizabeth Corley. Even though I was still sore about the way things went down for me at Beach City Top 40, I was ready for the challenge of this new station.

My first day at Midwest Music FM was February 2. It was a cold day with light snow. Already, I missed the Beach City sunshine. I said goodbye to Carol, pulled my wool jacket tight, lifted my collar against the wind, and got into my car to drive to work.

I found a place to park my Camaro right in front of the station. I took the elevator up with the anticipation of a kid on the first day of school. For a few seconds, I looked at the brightly painted logo on the glass door to the station. Then I opened the door to a new chapter of my life in radio.

"Hi, can I help you?"

A pretty, blonde receptionist wearing a tight red turtleneck and bright pink lipstick greeted me. I took off my winter jacket, tucked it under my arm, and extended my hand.

"Yeah, hi! I'm Donnie Dixon, the new program director. I'm here to see the general manager, Gordon Taylor."

"I'm Claudia. It's nice to meet you. Mr. Taylor is expecting you. I'll buzz him right now."

A minute or two later, the door behind her desk opened. Out came a middle-aged man with glasses and a moustache. He was wearing a tweed jacket and charcoal wool slacks.

"Hello, Donnie. I'm Gordon Taylor. Welcome to Midwest Music FM. Come on back into my office."

I followed him inside and took a seat on the other side of his expansive, polished desk. I looked around his office. It was sparsely decorated with the usual accoutrements. There were pictures of his pretty wife and children, a few books, and a globe on the shelf behind him.

Taylor was new to the Harkins chain, and I knew him only by his reputation. He seemed too old to be running a Top 40 radio station; he was in his mid-fifties. He was slightly paunchy with a graying moustache and a streak of silver in his hair.

"Welcome to the cold, not-so-sunny Midwest," he said. "How was the drive here?"

"It wasn't bad; we stopped to see the Grand Canyon."

"Are you and your wife getting settled?" he asked.

"Yeah. We're still at the hotel, but she's looking at apartments today, so we can get our son enrolled in school."

"You have a son?"

"Yeah, he's in second grade."

"I have two children, teenagers. They're a challenge."

"I'm sure."

"Donnie, I'm going to tell you something right up front. We don't have the same budget as Beach City Top 40. We have to do things on a smaller scale. We can't do as many contests, but I want you to plan a version of Ben Bailey's Best Contest for May."

"Good. That will be fun. What else is in the budget?"

"I can get you stickers, T-shirts, and buttons. We can always partner with the record companies for free concert tickets and backstage passes. And we can give away small cash prizes, like fifty-dollar bills."

Chicken feed. I thought.

"That sounds good," I said. What else was I going to say? That it sounded shitty?

"And once a year, during the sweeps, we do one big contest with a hefty grand prize. And we have a station van."

"I can do a lot with that," I said. "We can have the van cruise around the city. We'll distribute stickers that say 'I listen to Midwest Music in my car,' and give out cash prizes to people who have stickers on their cars or trucks."

"I like it. Come on. I'll show you your office."

When I saw the office, I was deeply disappointed, but of course I couldn't say anything. It was small, and I had to share it with a secretary. The room had two desks facing each other, two chairs, some shelves, and a cabinet. There were two phones, a record player in the corner, and not much else. At least there was a window with a view of the city. There was a large pile of unopened mail on one of the desks, and a stack of trade journals beside it. Clearly, no one had touched anything since the last program director had moved on.

"No secretary?" I asked.

"No, you'll have to hire someone. The last girl left about three weeks ago when her husband was transferred. You can hire whoever you like."

"Good," I said. "What about DJs? Harkins said I could bring one or two from Beach City. You're okay with that, right?"

"We're pretty well staffed right now. We have Mack Berger on morning drive and Danny Martin mid-mornings. Tony Parker is doing afternoons. He says you know him."

Unfortunately, I did. We'd worked together a few years ago, back when I was a jock in Atlanta. Tony was a skinny, muscular dude who came from Alabama. Back when I knew him, he had a wicked cocaine habit and chased anything in a skirt. He always had a super-hot girlfriend and another on the side.

"Oh, yeah, I know Tony. He's the best."

"Then there's Steve Sullivan doing evenings, and Stan Wilson doing overnights. Steve is a fucking genius if you don't mind my French. One day he'll be your boss. You'll meet him; he has shoulder-length brown hair and wire-rim John Lennon glasses. You'll like him, but I've got to warn you." He paused and lowered his voice. "He likes guys, not girls. He's a faggot."

I just nodded.

"But he has a way to help out the station. You'll see."

I didn't want to touch that one.

"Stan is a Negro, but he's one of our best. We have him since a large percent of our audience is Negro. He's a got an Afro and tortoise-shell glasses. We get away with paying him less, but don't ever let him know."

It figures, I thought.

"The last two guys are Randy Reed and Howie Brown. Randy does fill-ins and weekends. Howie does engineering and some production. He's our college boy. He told me he wants to go to grad school for broadcasting and communications. You'll meet them all soon."

"Good. So, are you saying that I can call in a couple of my jocks from Beach City?"

Gordon frowned and spread his hands. "The schedule is full, but I can put your top two guys at the top of the replacement list. If someone leaves, your guy can step in."

"But Harkins said—"

Gordon interrupted me with a growl in his voice. "Donnie, if Harkins or Elizabeth or Nick orders me to, I'll hire a goddamned gerbil. But until I get that order, I run this station. Got that?"

"Sure, Gordon," I said. "Honestly, no offense intended."

"None taken." Gordon looked at me intently. "Now, about Jackie. She's a different story. I have an express order to have you hire her as your music director next month."

"That's great, Gordon," I said.

"Yeah. It is." Gordon's voice grew stern. "But things are going to be different. She's my girl now. That's the official word."

"I see."

"Good. Now, listen. We're the number one Top 40 station in this market. Our only direct competition is Rivertown Radio. That station is run by Art Fields, who's a son of a bitch who would burn down our studio and kidnap your kids if he thought he could get away with it. Right now, we've got a nice lead in market share over Rivertown. Your job is to double that lead and leave that bastard Fields in the dust. Understand?"

"Yes."

"Good. Okay, Donnie, go get started. Knock our socks off."

I'd been at Midwest Music FM for less than an hour, and it was already clear to me there were only two kinds of people at this station: predators and prey.

27

Tuesday, August 10, 1976
Billboard Hot 100 Hit Song of the Week:
"Don't Go Breaking My Heart" by Elton John and Kiki Dee

After I got settled at Midwest Music, the first thing I had to do was find a secretary. I hired Marlene, a divorcee with a six-year-old son. She had big boobs and a great ass, but she was too old and too smart to use as a honeypot. That was a big plus for me. I didn't want to bring on anyone else who Gordon Taylor, Henry Harkins, or the Organization would want to pimp out.

Jackie arrived in March and began her new duties as music director. On Mondays she made phone calls to the record stores for sales figures, and added the top sellers to the request line favorites in her weekly report. On Tuesdays, she called Elizabeth Corley to finalize the song list. The rest of the time, she talked to promo guys and trade journals, and did special projects, like typing labels for the carts. Occasionally she took pictures, but the budget at Midwest Music was too tight to publish something like Beach City's *Hit Sheet*.

The highlight of April was a visit by Cheech and Chong. They did a bit on-air and recorded promos for us. Jackie took pictures for the trades. That night, their promo man threw a party for the jocks where Cheech and Chong showed up and did a comedy skit.

In May we did a version of Ben Bailey's Best Contest. I called it the Dream Prize Contest, and we touted it as a chance to win the prize of your dreams. The jocks helped me brainstorm 98 different prize packages, although the winner only got one. I convinced Gordon to let me spend $1000 on Ben Bailey, and he and I wrote the daily promos. It was a lot of fun. In the end, a teenage winner picked the Rolls Royce as his prize, but I convinced him to take ten thousand dollars to buy a sports car, saving the station three grand. What's a teenager going to do with a Rolls Royce anyway?

Unfortunately, even here in the Midwest, the jocks still had to deliver messages over the air. Each time I would get the word or phrase from Gordon Taylor, and the jocks would fit it into their patter. For a while, the code was simple—we just used the words, "it's true." Once meant something, twice meant something else. I still had no idea what those messages meant, or who they were for.

In June, Stan Wilson left for a higher-paying job in Chicago, and Gordon let me add a jock . I hired Kenny King. He arrived with his new wife, Christine.

On the Fourth of July, the entire staff and their families went to a swim party at Gordon Taylor's fancy house in the suburbs. I was impressed. Plus, I got to look at all the station chicks in their swimsuits. I don't know whether Carol noticed.

The band Heart visited the station later in July to push their latest single and do an on-air appearance. Their promo man was hitting on Jackie big-time, and I admit I got a little jealous. But I was smitten with sisters Ann and Nancy Wilson—enough to add their new hit, "Magic Man," to the play list. Fortunately, it soon became a mega-hit.

In August, we did something that had never been done before on a Harkins radio station. One of our jocks, Randy Reed, created a 52-hour music special called the Imagination Concert. Randy put together live versions of top songs from albums and concert tapes, added sound effects, and created the longest and best—but simulated—live concert ever performed. We just played it this last weekend, so everyone else could take some time off. It was a smash.

So that brings us up to today. It was almost quitting time, and Marlene and I were chatting about the upcoming three-day Labor Day telethon when the phone rang. I picked up.

"Donnie Dixon speaking."

"Donnie, it's Elizabeth"

Shit. "What's up, Elizabeth?"

"I have something important to discuss. Are you alone?"

"I'm sitting here with Marlene, going over the plans for the Labor Day weekend remote, and rehashing the Imagination Concert."

"I have something serious to discuss. Tell Marlene to go home and close the door."

I did as she said and braced myself.

"Okay, I'm alone. What are we getting paid to play this week, Elizabeth?"

"This isn't about music, Donnie, it's something else. Over the Labor Day weekend, you're going to do some entertaining. This will be for two of Mr. Harkins' local friends."

"Organization men?" I asked.

"Yes."

"Listen closely, Donnie. This is the plan. It's going down at Tony's house."

"Tony Parker, my afternoon jock?"

"Yeah, Tony. The pretext is a station party. Have Tony only invite jocks who are onboard with the program. At the right time, Tony will give the signal, the jocks will leave, and then the private party will start. Jackie will be the guest of honor."

Of course she will.

"I can't be there," Elizabeth said, "but I'm sending a colleague. His name is Ray. You haven't met him yet."

I bet he's a real ray of sunshine.

The words came out of me before I could stop them: "Again? When are you going to leave that poor girl alone?"

Elizabeth hissed, "Why do you think we brought Jackie to Midwest Music? For that matter, why do you think we brought *you*? Shut up and listen."

"Alright, I'm listening."

"Have one of your jocks invite her. She's still friends with Kenny, right?"

"Right."

"And she still takes pictures for special events, doesn't she?"

"Yeah."

"So, tell her to take pictures at the telethon early Saturday night, when Steve Sullivan is on the air. Then have Kenny invite her to the party at Tony's. He can convince her to drive to Tony's and park her car so they can go and return together. Kenny can help Tony with Jackie, but he has to split as soon as she's knocked out.

"Why are you doing this at Tony's? I asked. "He's just a 27-year-old jock. He's nothing special."

"That's what he looks like to you, Donnie. But you have no idea who Tony really is."

What the hell? "Who is he, then?"

Elizabeth laughed. "Do you think I'm gonna tell *you*? *You're* the one who's nothing special. Donnie, you don't know who his father is—and this is something his father asked for."

"But Elizabeth, it's one thing to have Jackie pimped out to guys she's never gonna see again. Are you telling me you want me to pimp her out to somebody she's gonna have to see every day in the office?"

Elizabeth's tone was hard as stone. "First of all, Donnie, I'm not pimping her out to Tony. It's just at his house. Let me finish."

"Okay."

"Listen again closely, Donnie. This is the plan. Instruct Kenny to get Jackie to Tony's for the party. Have Tony invite three other jocks so it looks authentic. You know which guys we can trust."

"Yeah; Mack, Randy, and Howie, they're on the inside."

"Pay them off, Donnie," said Elizabeth. "Twenties should do it."

"No problem," I said.

"Have Tony make it a normal station party. Beers, chips, pot, whatever. Nick will send you the drugs and you'll give them to Tony in advance. Around eleven-thirty, have Tony tell everyone it's time to call it a night. That's the cue. Have him ask Jackie if she has cotton mouth and offer her a soda for the ride home. He'll give her the spiked soda and usher the jocks out. Kenny can stay a few minutes longer to help. Tell him not to let the others see her collapse on the couch. Like I said, tell Tony to make sure Kenny splits as soon as Jackie's asleep. You should get there right around midnight. Ray and the Organization guests will arrive a little later and the real party will begin."

"And then?"

"You're the ringmaster and the bouncer, Donnie. Also, the photographer, just like before. Buy a Polaroid with petty cash from the station. Make sure everything goes as planned. When the party is over and everyone leaves, get

Jackie dressed, get her back on the couch, and cover her with a blanket. Then your job is done, and you can split. When she wakes up in the morning, have Tony tell her she passed out on the couch. Tell him to give her some coffee and send her home. Is that clear, Donnie?"

"Clear as a bell," I said grimly. "Anything else?"

Elizabeth's tone softened slightly. "Yes. This is a big deal. We're trusting you with a lot, and we expect you to do it right."

I couldn't stop myself. "Why are you doing this, Elizabeth?"

"I'm doing this because Henry Harkins told me to. *You* do what *I* tell *you* to do. *I* do what Henry tells *me* to do. Understand?" She paused and waited. "Do you, Donnie?"

"I do."

"Jackie will be fine. She won't remember a thing."

Without saying goodbye, Elizabeth hung up.

28

Saturday, August 21, 1976
Billboard Hot 100 Hit Song of the Week:
"Don't Go Breaking My Heart" by Elton John and Kiki Dee

After the call from Elizabeth, I told Jackie to take pictures on the Saturday of the Labor Day remote, and she easily agreed. She always did everything I told her to do. Next, I had to line things up with Kenny and Tony. I made plans with Tony to stop by his place in the late afternoon, and I figured I could grab Kenny on the way out of the station.

I finished some production work around the same time Kenny finished his shift, planning it so it looked natural to walk out of the station together. He didn't know it was an ambush.

"Kenny, dude, great show today," I said, heading toward the door .

"Thanks man."

I continued in the elevator. "There's something I need to talk to you about, man. Can I walk with you to your car?"

"No problemo, what's up?" he said.

We talked about station stuff until we got outside, then I hit him up.

"Kenny, I need your help with something," I said.

"Is this about Jackie?" he said, no doubt remembering Beach City, "You can always count on me."

"You two are still friends, right?"

"Yeah, we're still friends."

"So she'll listen to you."

"I think so," he said.

"This job isn't hard or anything," I said.

We turned the corner toward his Ford Pinto, so I just spit it out. "Jackie's going to be the guest of honor at a little station party at Tony's on the Saturday of the Labor Day telethon. I already told her she needs to take pictures at the remote. Your job is to get her to the party," I said. "If you invite her, she won't want to miss it. Then, casually, explain it would be easier for her to drive to Tony's and go together. Afterward you'll drive her back for the party. I just need her to be there. The fun won't begin until later."

"The fun?" Kenny asked.

"Just keep listening, Kenny. Tony's house is close to the shopping center, so she won't suspect anything, and if she rides with you, she won't drive home," I said.

"Okay, but what kind of party is this supposed to be? Why does Jackie have to be there?"

I raised the pitch of my voice. "Seriously Kenny? Don't question me. It's a station party, that's all you need to know. Tony will invite some of the jocks. Pass around some joints and drink some beer. Just act like you're at a regular station party."

We arrived at Kenny's car.

"Does this have something to do with what happened at Capri Island?" he asked.

"Something like that, Kenny," I said. "But it isn't your job to ask questions. Your job is to do what I tell you to do. Got it?" I was getting exasperated, and Kenny could tell.

"Kenny, since you need to know, I'm gonna tell you. Tony's going to give Jackie a drink to make her fall asleep. You'll help Tony get her into the bedroom, and then you'll split."

He finally saw the light. "Oh," he said, " Now I get it."

He unlocked the driver's side and got in. I put one hand on the door and told him in the most menacing voice I could muster.

"Kenny, I want you to know you can go far in this organization if you follow orders. These are your orders: Invite Jackie to the party. Convince Jackie to meet you at Tony's house. Go together to the remote so she can take pictures. Drive her back. Make sure she stays at the party with the jocks. When Tony says to help him, help him. When Tony says to leave, leave. That's all you have to do. Got it?"

He shook his head slowly up and down, and I knew he'd go along. "Got it."

"Okay. Get back to me later if you have any questions," I said.

I shut his car door and watched him drive off . Then I walked two blocks back to my Camaro.

It took twenty minutes to drive to Tony's. He rented a small rancher in a quiet residential neighborhood that was close to the shopping center where we were going to do the Labor Day weekend remote.

Tony was waiting for me by the front door, and let me right in. It was another August scorcher. Thankfully, Tony had central air. I surveyed the modest furnishings, while Tony went to grab me a beer.

"Make yourself comfortable," he yelled from the kitchen.

"Nice place, dude," I said when he returned with a cold one. He pulled a chair up next to where I settled on the couch.

"It's nothing fancy," he said. "Just the basics." A jock never stays too long in any one place. That was a given in radio.

"As long as you've got a bangin' stereo," I said, as I looked at his high-end equipment tuned to our station. It was stacked on an etagere against the opposite wall. The shelves were filled with hundreds of records, and the top shelf had a few pictures and knick-knacks from different radio stations.

"How's that girlfriend of yours? Laura, isn't that her name?"

"She's great, she'll be over in an hour." he said.

One thing about Tony, he had three loves. Radio, blow, and pussy.

"So, Tony, do you know why I'm here?"

"Something to do with a party?" he said. "I already heard a little bit through the grapevine."

"Yeah man, you heard right. I'm here because I need to explain everything outside of the station. This is important."

"Don't stress it, man. Here, let's light one up and discuss." Tony just happened to have a rolled joint sitting in a large ashtray on the coffee table. I wasn't gonna say no.

He lit it up, inhaled and passed it to me. I took a long hit and gave it back to Tony. For a few moments, my thoughts drifted, but then I focused.

"This is how it's going down," I said. "You're gonna have a small station party, on Saturday, September 4th, and Jackie is the guest of honor."

"Jackie, that hippie chick, *her*?" he said. "She's a weirdo."

"Yeah, Jackie," I said. "Now don't ask questions, this is straight from the top, from Henry Harkins himself. Listen carefully, okay?"

"Yeah, sure, whatever," Tony took the last hit, held it in, nodded, exhaled, then stubbed the roach into the ashtray. I lit up a cig and passed another to Tony.

"I already told Jackie she has to take pictures at the remote. I just finished giving Kenny his instructions. I told him the same thing I'm telling you . The station party is the cover story . Kenny will invite Jackie to your house for a small party with a few of the jocks . I'm inviting Mack, Randy, and Howie; we can trust them. I'll fill them in with the details so they know what to expect. Everyone will know to act like it's a regular party, but when you give the signal, they all have to split . That way you and Kenny will be alone with Jackie for the operation . Kenny can stay a few minutes extra if you need help. I trust him."

"Operation?" he said. "What are we gonna do?"

"You only have one job, Tony, and that's to give Jackie a soda."

"A soda, that's easy," he said.

"Here." I reached in my pocket and pulled out a small packet. I handed it over.

"What's this?" Tony asked.

"It's the powder, stupid. Jackie isn't going to be awake for the party."

"Oh, yeah, right," he nodded.

Getting serious, I thrust a finger at Tony, "You don't understand how important this is. Listen. At some point near the end of the night, Jackie will get cotton mouth. She might even get up and say she's going to leave. That's when you spring into action. Tell her you'll get her a soda for the road. Go in the kitchen, get the can, and pour in the whole packet of powder. Shake it around a little bit until it dissolves and bring it to her."

"What if she won't drink it?" Tony argued.

"She'll drink it. Don't worry, she'll be thirsty. Tell her the caffeine will keep her awake for the drive home. And Tony, make sure she drinks the whole thing."

"What's Kenny gonna do?"

"He'll just stay a few minutes longer so Jackie doesn't get suspicious. Around eleven-thirty you'll signal the party's over, and the jocks have to leave. Give Jackie the drink, and you and Kenny make sure she's sitting on the couch. When she falls asleep, you two drag her into the bedroom. Then get rid of Kenny and wait for me . I'll be there around midnight, and the other guests will arrive a little later."

"Other guests?" Tony said.

"Oh, quit playing dumb, you know what this is about." I said. "Yeah, you're right, who's coming?"

"I'll be there, and a guy named Ray, he's an associate of Elizabeth Corley. Plus, two other guys."

"Yeah, I think I know who they are."

"What?" I said, surprised.

"Donnie, in case no one has told you, I'm connected. Well, my father is. That's why this party is at my place. I'll check with him."

"Shit," I said.

"I don't care how connected you are, Tony, you can't screw this up."

"Donnie, don't you get it? They're doing this as a favor for someone. Everything will be fine."

"It's not gonna be fine unless we are careful." Now I was starting to get afraid. "If something goes wrong, we could all go to jail."

Tony laughed, "No one is going to jail, Donnie. My father has friends. No one ever goes to jail."

"Who the hell is your father, Tony?

"You don't know who my father is, Donnie, but he knows everything about you."

Great, I thought, this crap is just getting deeper and deeper.

"Okay, dude, you know how it's going down." I stubbed out my cig, put down my beer, and got up. "I'm going home for dinner. See you on Monday."

Tony walked me to the door. "'Bye Donnie, and don't worry, nothing will go wrong."

29

Wednesday, August 25, 1976
Billboard Hot 100 Hit Song of the Week:
"Don't Go Breaking My Heart" by Elton John and Kiki Dee

I was surrounded by evil on all sides. I had had enough. It was time to make my move.

I waited until just before 5:00, when I had the office to myself. Nobody was around except Steve Sullivan in the control booth. I picked up the phone, took a deep breath, and dialed.

"Rivertown Radio. How may I help you?"

"Art Fields, please," I said. My hand holding the receiver was shaking.

"One moment, please."

"Fields," a gruff voice said.

"This is Donnie Dixon."

"And who are you?"

Shit. I knew the names of his key people. I'd hoped that he knew the names of Gordon's.

"I'm the program director at Midwest Music FM."

That must have shocked him, because for a couple of seconds he was silent.

Finally, he said, "Okay. Tell me why you're calling."

"I have something to sell you."

"What is it?" he asked.

"Research."

There was another pause. Then Art said, "One of those WKR Radio books? With all the data from our market?"

"Yeah."

"The current one?"

"Uh-huh."

"You're shittin' me," he said.

"I'm not. It's not the original, of course. I'll make you a Xerox copy."

Fields grunted. "Okay, how much?"

"A thousand. And I can get you a new one every two months, as they come out."

"Five hundred per book."

"Only 500 bucks?"

"That's six grand a year. That's what the books are worth to me. Take it or leave it."

I sat there, thinking. I'd expected Fields to jump at the chance to get his hands on the books. I hadn't expected him to bargain. Was it worth risking my career for $6000 a year?

"Isn't Harkins paying you enough?" Fields asked.

"Not for what he wants me to do."

Fields laughed. "I get it," he said. "Is it a deal?"

What the hell, I thought. "Deal. Payment in cash, of course."

"Uh huh. Have a courier deliver the book to the station on Monday. They can pick up a package at the same time with the money in it. What name should I address it to?"

I thought for a moment. "E. R. Murrow."

Fields snorted. "Cut the crap."

"Address it to me."

Fields snorted. "Fine."

"How do I know you're going to actually pay me?"

"How do I know that this conversation isn't bullshit, and your piece-of-shit boss isn't just paying you to bust my balls?"

Now it was my turn to laugh. "I'm for real, Mr. Fields. I'm going to trust that you are, too."

I thought we were finished, but Art wasn't. "One more thing," he said.

"What?"

"I know all about Jackie."

Damn, this is getting complicated. "What do you mean?"

"Harkins told me himself. He was bragging."

"When did you talk to him?"

"I talk to him every so often. We have friends in common."

That stopped me cold.

"Pimping out his own employees." Fields said. "And the knockout drugs. And the black magic. And then bragging about it. Harkins is a piece of work."

I was too stunned to speak.

But Fields wasn't finished. He said, "And all of it just to raise some money. He told me he was looking for a European investor. Jackie was the party favor."

The European investor. That had to be the guy in Palm Springs.

"If Jackie were my daughter," Fields said, "I'd shoot that bastard Harkins dead, and feel proud for doing it."

I didn't know what to say to that, so I kept silent.

"Word travels fast and far in this business," Fields told me. "So, you and I need to keep our arrangement strictly confidential. No bragging and no hinting to anyone. Not to your best friend. Not to your wife, if you have one. Got that?"

"Got it."

"Okay, I'll get the money together over the weekend. Send me the package on Monday."

"Listen, Art, about Jackie—"

But Fields had hung up.

30

Saturday, September 4, 1976
Billboard Hot 100 Hit Song of the Week:
"You Should Be Dancing" by The Bee Gees

I got to Tony's around eleven-thirty and drove past his house to check the cars. I wanted to see which of the jocks had left. Jackie's blue Honda Civic was there, so I knew she was inside. I parked at the end of the block and turned off my engine and lights. I lit up a cig while I watched the jocks leave, one by one, until everyone was gone. It was almost midnight when I grabbed the Polaroid, got out of the car, and walked up to Tony's door. I didn't need to ring the bell. He was waiting to let me in.

I nodded hello, and closing the door behind me I asked Tony, "Is she asleep?"

"She's on the bed, passed out like Sleeping Beauty," he said.

"Good," I said, and walked over to the kitchen, where I put the camera on the kitchen counter.

Walking back into the living room I told Tony, "I'm gonna take a look."

I walked to the bedroom door, opened it, and glanced inside. She was laid out on the bed, still dressed, and asleep.

Satisfied, I shut the door and went back into the living room, where Tony had lit a cigarette, and was making a feeble attempt at cleaning up.

"Was it hard getting her in there?" I asked.

"Nah, she sucked down that soda and was o.u.t. in minutes. I got rid of the jocks, and me and Kenny dragged her into the bedroom," he said. "Then Kenny split."

"Yeah, I saw him leave."

I took out another cig for myself, lit it up, and asked Tony. "Did she drink the whole soda?"

"Yeah, I think so," Tony replied. But then he picked up a can from the coffee table, "This was hers." He shook it and replied, "Um, no. She only drank half."

"Let me have that," I grabbed it away from him and put it in the kitchen next to the camera. I hoped the dose was enough. I returned to the living room and stood there with Tony, finishing our smokes, with a queasy feeling in the pit of my stomach, not knowing what would happen next.

There was a knock at Tony's door. He opened it, and in front of us stood a sinister figure. He was a tall, muscular guy, with black hair, a pointed goatee, and bloodshot eyes. He was holding an oversized, scuffed, leather satchel.

"You must be Ray," I said, and let him in.

He put down the satchel and extended his tattooed right hand, "Yeah. Who the hell are you?"

"Donnie," I answered, "And this is Tony. This is his place."

Tony attempted to hold out his hand to shake, but Ray ignored him.

Ray sniffed and wiped his nose with his sleeve, he must have been high on something, "I know your dad, you look just like him."

Tony looked bewildered. This was a side of the boisterous jock I hadn't seen. Then I took a closer look at Ray's eyes.

They were glazed over. I attempted to talk to him, but he just pushed me aside.

"Show me the chick," he demanded, his eyes darting around the room.

"She's in the bedroom," I said.

I tried to be accommodating, but this guy wasn't playing nice. He picked up his satchel and walked right into Tony's bedroom.

He turned around and told us, "I'll come out when she's ready." Then he shut the bedroom door.

I went into the kitchen with Tony, and I tried to get some information out of him.

"Tony," I said, "We've been friends for a long time, but I don't really know much about your family. Who is your dad, anyway?"

"He's kind of a big shot, he owns a construction company," Tony said. "And some of his biggest accounts are local businesses. My dad knows everybody and everything in this town.

"Yeah, I see," I said, putting two and two together. The Organization.

"He told me about this party, and how important it is."

"For you or for him?" I asked.

"Actually, for me." He just let that hang there. "In my father's world it's all about respect and trust. And doing favors, that's what this is. The chick is a nothin' but party favor."

"I see," I nodded, in other words, a honeypot.

"Donnie, this whole thing is making me nervous. I just want it to be over. Do you want to do some lines while we wait?" said Tony.

"Sure, man," I said.

Tony pulled out his stash of coke from his pocket and laid out two lines on the countertop. We each snorted a line, sucked down our beers, and waited.

Just before one, there was a soft knock at the door. The Organization men. Before we went to answer, I had to establish one thing with Tony.

"Tony, I want you to promise me something."

"What is it, Donnie?"

"Whatever happens, whatever noises you hear, I want you to promise to stay out of the bedroom and leave Jackie alone. Promise?"

"Yeah, dude, I promise. I'll leave her alone. I gotta hot girlfriend, remember? I don't need that shit."

"Okay," I said. "You stay in the living room and keep watch. Afterward we'll get her dressed and back on the couch. Let her wake up in the morning like nothing happened. When she wakes up, tell her she passed out, give her coffee, and send her home. Agreed?"

"Agreed," he replied.

We both went to the front door and Tony opened it. The moon cast an eerie light over the dark neighborhood. The only noise was a dog barking a couple of houses down. The two Organization men came in. I put my finger in front of my lips, motioning them to be quiet until we got to the kitchen.

Tony and I introduced ourselves.

I went first. "I'm Donnie, I'm the program director for Midwest Music," I said, and nodding toward Tony, "Tony is our number one disc jockey, I think you know his father."

The bigger guy offered his hand, "I'm Johnnie, good to know you, man." He grabbed mine and squeezed it tight. "I dig what you're doing at the station. I listen in my car."

"Dude," said Tony, extending his hand.

Then Johnnie touched his companion's arm, "This is Carmen." Carmen nodded and gave me a limp shake. He nodded at Tony.

"Yeah, we know Tony's dad," said Carmen.

"Tony told me," I said.

Johnnie wore a pinstriped navy three-piece suit buttoned tightly over his midsection. He must have come from some fancy bar. Carmen was a skinny, wiry, dude in glasses, wearing a light-colored shirt and pants. They both wore expensive leather shoes and those popular, flashy gold chains.

The guys didn't seem half bad. I wondered why they participated in such dirty business. I looked at them more carefully. Johnnie had a broad forehead, a large upper body, thick legs, and his breath smelled like liquor. Aviator glasses accentuated Carmen's deep-set eyes.

Introductions finished, I said, "It's almost time. Ray is in the bedroom with the chick. He'll come out when he's ready. Meanwhile, you guys want some blow? How 'bout some beers?"

Carmen spoke up, "Yeah, man."

We pulled up chairs around the small kitchen table while Tony handed out beers from the fridge. I pulled my stash and a razor blade out of my cigarette pack and put six lines on the kitchen table. Johnnie expertly rolled up a ten and proceeded to fill each nostril. He handed the bill to Carmen who snorted one line, and then to me, and then to Tony, who finished them up.

I needed another cig and pulled one out of my pack, automatically passing another to Tony. Despite the air conditioning, he was starting to sweat. We all waited, lost in our own thoughts, in anticipation of what was going to happen next.

Tony got up and started to pace around the small room.

"Chill out, Tony. Sit down. Ray will be out soon."

"Who's this Ray guy?" asked Johnnie.

"He's in charge of the fun stuff, you'll see him in a minute," I said.

Johnnie, turned to me. "You're gonna take pictures, aren't you?"

"Me and Johnnie need pictures," said Carmen.

"No worries, I've got a Polaroid camera right here." I pointed to it sitting on the kitchen counter.

Finally, the door to the bedroom opened. Ray had changed into a black-hooded robe. I noticed his left ear was pierced with a small gold ring. and he had tattoos on both hands that went up his arms. On his right hand, was a ring like Elizabeth's, only his had a huge black stone. His fingernails were dirty, and his breath smelled like cigarettes.

"The girl is ready," he said. "She is the Bride of the Beast."

"What?" I asked.

"She's our sacrifice. You may enter now."

With a flourish, Ray led the three of us into Tony's bedroom.

When I saw Jackie, I gasped.

She was out cold, stark naked, and tied up spread-eagle on the bed, with a red pentagram painted on her stomach. Her head was resting to the side, with her curly light brown hair arranged on her bare shoulders. Drops of something red were on her forehead.

Behind the bed was Tony's nightstand. On it were incense, three black candles, a wand, a chalice, and a dagger. Ray's clothes were in a heap in the corner.

The Organization men were behind me. I couldn't tell if they were filled with horror, lust, or a combination of the two. They had blasé expressions, like they had seen this many times before.

It was time to begin. He motioned us into position.

"Stand in the circle," he instructed, "but do not step inside the triangle of power."

There was a large circle in chalk on the carpeted floor around the bed. Inside the circle, behind the head of the bed, was a chalk triangle. Tony's nightstand was pushed inside the triangle; Ray stood behind it. He took a lighter out of a robe pocket, lit the incense and candles, and picked up the dagger.

Holding the dagger high in the air, he intoned, "I burn the black flames to honor Satan and the hosts of hell. I conjure the spirits of Beelzebub, Baphomet, Lucifer, and Satan. I strongly command thee to appear."

Using the dagger, he traced the shapes of a cross and a pentagram in the air in front of him. Then he touched the dagger to his forehead, chest, right shoulder, and left shoulder.

"To thee... the kingdom... the power... the glory... for all the ages... Amen."

As if by instinct, every one of us said, "Amen."

Ray crossed his arms. "Before me, Raphael; behind me, Gabriel; on my right, Michael; and on my left, Ariel." As he spoke, he turned in a circle. I could see his eyes were closed.

He opened his eyes and made the cross and the pentagram in the air again with the dagger. "Around me are the flames of the Dark Lord. Amen."

We all repeated, "Amen."

"I do invoke, conjure, and command the spirits of Beelzebub, Baphomet, Lucifer, and Satan to appear quickly and show themselves in the circle."

Then he put the dagger back on the altar, picked up the wand, and raised his arms in the air.

"Amen... Evil from us deliver but... Temptation into not us lead and... Us against trespass who those forgive we as... Trespasses our us forgive and... Bread daily our day this us give... Heaven in is it as earth on... Done be will thy... Come kingdom thy... Name thy be hallowed... Heaven in art who... Father our."

It was the Lord's Prayer, backward.

The room got cold, and time stood still. I saw a glow above the bed, but it quickly faded away. I felt something unholy fill the room.

Ray continued his invocation: "In the name of Satan, ruler of Earth, the King of the world, I command the forces of darkness to bestow their infernal power upon us and open wide the gates of hell. Come forth from the abyss to bless this unholy treatise!"

Ray replaced the wand on the altar and picked up something small I hadn't noticed before. It was a sharp sewing needle. He walked over to Jackie, lifted her left hand, and pricked her middle finger.

Then he opened the front of his robe, revealing his small, very erect cock. He picked up her flaccid arm and smeared the blood dripping from her finger over his erection.

He bent down and whispered in her ear. "You won't remember any of this. You won't remember a thing."

No one in the room moved. The only motion was the gentle flickering of the candles.

"She is the Bride of the Beast," Ray suddenly shouted. Then he threw off his robe, mounted Jackie, and thrust his engorged cock deep inside her. He pounded himself against her and pulled on her pale breasts. Now I could see the black tattoos that covered most of his arms and back. "Magnus Satanus, Magnus Satanus, Magnus Satanus," he growled. He thrust into her, harder and faster, finally screaming "Magnus Satanus!" one more time as he had his climax.

Then he dismounted the poor girl, put on his black robe, and pointed at Johnnie.

"Now, you may take your turn."

"Me?" squeaked Johnnie.

"Yes."

The big guy pulled off his trousers, boxers, and jacket and stood in front of Jackie in just his shirt and vest. He had thick hairy legs, a fat stomach, and a short, semi-erect cock. Perspiration dripped down his face. He didn't seem to know what to do next.

Solemnly, Ray walked over and squeezed Jackie's finger to get a drop of blood. Then he smeared it on Johnnie's cock. He nodded in Jackie's direction. "Go ahead," he said in a low growl. "Now."

Sweating, Johnnie knelt over her, held down her arms, climbed on top of her, and began thrusting.

I didn't want to watch, but I had to take pictures. I took a few Polaroids of Johnnie on top of Jackie. Then, looked down at my shoes, I heard Johnnie's grunts and the rhythmic rumble of the moving bed.

After a minute or two, I dared to look up. Johnnie was having trouble keeping his cock inside her and kept shoving it in with his hand.

Eventually he finished and got up. He bent down and pulled a handkerchief out of his jacket, wiped his forehead and his penis, and put all his clothes back on. He slunk to the back of the room and stood against the wall.

Then Ray pointed to Carmen. "Now you." I got my camera ready again.

Carmen quickly stripped and threw his shirt and pants in a heap on the floor. He left the gold chain around his neck.

Again, Ray walked over and picked up Jackie's hand to squeeze out a tiny drop of blood and smear it on Carmen's cock. He got on the bed, pushed her legs open, and lay on top of her. After a few seconds, he got back up on his knees. I could see that he didn't have an erection. He reached down and stroked his cock until it got hard. When he finally entered her, he looked at me with wild eyes.

"Get the shot! Get the shot!"

I moved in close to get the picture and clicked the shutter. A flash of light filled the room.

"I got it," I said, softly.

Carmen thrust inside Jackie a few more times, then pulled out. He climbed next to her face, stroked himself a few quick times, and, with a grunt and a moan, ejaculated all over her neck and cheek. I took two more photos.

Carmen stood beside Jackie for a few seconds, breathing heavily. Then bent down and wiped off his cock with her thick, curly hair.

Carmen gathered up his clothes and dressed. He wiped his hands on the back of his pants, and then stood next to Johnnie, still panting.

Ray stepped behind his altar, where the black candles had almost burned out. The air was thick with the smell of incense. Ray raised his hands above his head to get our attention.

"Our ceremony is almost over. Come back to the circle and I will pass the chalice. All will drink."

We stepped back into place. Ray removed the chalice from the altar, took a sip, and passed it to me. It was rum, as before. I took a small sip and passed it to Carmen, who took a drink, and then to Johnnie, who did the same. When it was returned to Ray, he spoke again.

"The Beauty is now married to the Beast. We thank Beelzebub, Baphomet, Lucifer, and Satan. We drink from the goblet to honor Satan and the hosts of hell."

Raising both arms, he declared, "Hail Satan! Hail Satan!"

The rest of us stood still and silent.

Ray picked up the dagger and traced the shapes of a cross and a pentagram in the air in front of him. Then he touched the dagger to his forehead, chest, right shoulder and left shoulder.

"To thee... the Kingdom... the power... the glory... for all the ages... Amen." He looked at us, nodded, and said softly, like a minister to his flock, "Say with me."

"Amen," we all said together.

"I bind the demons and here do license them to depart unto their proper place, without causing harm or danger unto man or beast. Depart, then, I say, and be thou ready to come again at my call, being duly exorcised and conjured to the sacred rites of magic. I charge thee to withdraw, and the peace of God be ever continued between thee and me. Amen."

"Amen," we echoed.

Ray put down the dagger. "The ritual is now complete."

We all stood in the circle, not knowing what to do.

Then I felt an unmistakable *whoosh* of something other-worldly departing. It wasn't a thing I could see—just a feeling.

It was finally over. The whole ritual hadn't taken more than an hour.

I was ready to get the hell out of there. I hated having to take pictures, but at least this time I didn't have to participate.

Me, Johnnie, and Carmen filed out of the bedroom to join Tony in the kitchen. I heard Ray go into the bathroom. He needed to clean Jackie up. There was a strict rule not to mark her body or leave any telltale signs. I turned to Johnnie and Carmen.

"Did you get what you came for?" I asked.

"Yeah, man," replied Johnnie.

"Yeah," said Carmen. "That chick is hot. I wish I could date her."

"I don't think you're her type," I said, hoping Carmen couldn't hear the sarcasm in my voice. What a creep.

Ray appeared, dressed. I could still smell the smoke from the blown-out candles and the scent of the incense drifting in from the bedroom.

"Did you get all your stuff?" I asked.

"Yeah, it's in my satchel," Ray nodded.

"Is she cleaned up?" I asked him.

"Not a scratch," said Ray.

Carmen looked at Johnnie, indicating they were ready to split.

"We need those pictures," Carmen reminded me.

"Yeah, sure," I reached into my jeans pocket and handed them to Johnnie. He examined them, one at a time, and tucked them into his jacket.

Tony was still wired on coke, and started bugging me. "What happened in there, Donnie? Is Jackie alright? What the hell did you do? I was going crazy out here."

"Tony," I said, "I told you, this has nothing to do with you. Your job is almost over. Now all you have to do is keep your mouth shut. Get it?"

"Yeah," he answered.

"I'm gonna walk these guys out," I said. "Stay here in the kitchen, I'll be right back."

"Okay," said Tony.

Everyone grabbed their stuff and the four of us; me, Ray, Johnnie, and Carmen walked outside into the humid evening air. I pulled out a cig and watched the two Organization men get in their car and leave . I could only hope that I would never run into them again by accident.

That left me and Ray quietly standing outside. Ray pulled out his smokes and we stood there, looking at the stars.

"What we did was very powerful," he told me. "I had a whole coven back home doing black magic at the very same time."

A chill went through my body.

"Tell me Ray, why do you do this?" I was genuinely curious.

"It's my religion. It's my church." Ray said. "You'd be surprised how many of us there are."

"Really?"

"Yeah, my coven has 150 members and there are 9,000 of us in four states."

"Shit," I said.

"The coven is led by a guy who used to be a preacher," he said. "And another guy who works at a university. We have doctors and lawyers and all sorts of people."

I interrupted Ray. "I don't want to know anymore," I said. "Just tell Elizabeth we did everything she asked."

He threw his cig on the ground and stepped on it. "Okay dude, it's been real. See you next time." He picked up his stuff.

"Goodbye," I said. *I hope not.* I stubbed out my cig and watched him drive away. Then I went back in the house to finish things up.

When I walked back inside, Tony wasn't in the kitchen. He wasn't in the bathroom either. Without warning, I heard a Jackie screaming, followed by Tony's screams. This couldn't be happening. I was only gone a few minutes.

Abruptly, Tony ran out of the bedroom, stark naked, his erect cock flapping around.

"She woke up, Donnie, she woke up!" he screamed.

Jackie's screams continued and then turned into loud sobs.

"You promised me, you bastard. You weren't supposed to touch her," I bellowed.

"When you were outside, I peeked into the bedroom. I couldn't help myself," Tony explained.

"You're gonna get us arrested or worse, you fool!"

Tony's erection began to subside, and he began to bawl. "I just couldn't help myself…"

"Where's her drink?" I scanned the room and picked up Jackie's soda where I had left it in the kitchen. Jackie was still screaming and sobbing.

"Damn it, Tony, why did I trust you?"

"It's not my fault," said Tony, still naked.

Composing myself, I walked into the bedroom, carrying the half-drunk can of soda. Jackie had stopped sobbing and was quietly sniveling and starting to get dressed . She sat on the edge of the bed in her t-shirt and panties, looking for her jeans.

"Donnie, what are *you* doing here? What am *I* doing here? I woke up with Tony on top of me. I hate that guy." She started screaming again. "I hate him! I hate him!"

I didn't know what to do. I used my best jock voice and said, "Calm down, Jackie, everything will be fine. I'll take care of you, honey. Don't worry."

I sat down next to her on the edge of the bed. I put my arm around her shoulder and patted her head until she calmed down. Like a child, she rested her head on my shoulder and breathed some long, deep breaths. I handed her the half-finished can of soda.

"Here, drink the rest of this. I'll make sure you get back home."

She hadn't figured out the soda was drugged and obediently finished the can. It only took a few moments for her to fall back in the bed, knocked out again. I got up and went into the living room.

Tony had put his pants on by now and couldn't stop apologizing, "I couldn't help myself, Donnie, I just couldn't. I walked into my bedroom and there she was, naked in my bed. I got in beside her and put my arm around her. She was still knocked out, so I figured, why not a quickie?"

"Shut up, you asshole," I hissed. "You have no idea…"

I was sick to my stomach. Sick of him, of Henry Harkins, of Elizabeth Corley, of Midwest Music, of Gordon Taylor, the whole lot.

"I'm leaving!" I announced. "You figure out this mess!"

Tony meekly nodded.

I slammed the door behind me and walked down the block to my car.

It was almost 2:00 a.m., and I knew that in a few hours I was going to have my chain yanked hard. And that was if I was lucky. I didn't dare think of some of the other possibilities.

I lit up the last of my cigs to keep me awake. There was no way I was going to talk my way out of this one. Resigned, I turned on the stereo. The song playing was "Magic Man." I reached over to the radio and turned it off.

31

Tuesday, September 7, 1976
Billboard Hot 100 Hit Song of the Week:
"You Should Be Dancing" by The Bee Gees

The phone rang early on Tuesday morning. I picked it up. The moment I heard Gordon's voice, I knew I was in deep shit.

"Donnie, you pissant. My office, 9:00 a.m. sharp."

Before I could even say okay, he had hung up.

I looked at the clock. It was already seven-thirty.

I thought of the one guy I could trust—my buddy Vince. I dialed his number, hoping he'd be home. He answered on the second ring.

"Hello?"

"Hi, Vince. It's me, Donnie. Did I wake you?"

"No, I'm about to leave for the office. What's up?"

"We threw a party for some VIPs and something went wrong."

"Damn. What happened?"

"One of the guys didn't follow orders. He was having too much fun."

"And?"

"Jackie—our honeypot—woke up in the DJ's bed," I said. "With him on top of her."

"Shit."

"Gordon already called me. He wants to see me at nine."

"Uh-huh." Then silence.

"What do you think I should do?" I asked.

There was another moment of silence. Then Vince said, "Face the music. Take your lumps."

"What do you think that will mean?"

More silence for a few seconds. "I dunno," Vince said sadly. "End of your career, probably, if you're lucky. The Organization has murdered people for less."

Holy shit. "Christ. You think Harkins will have me killed?"

"Not likely. Not if Gordon took the trouble to call you into his office. But your meeting with him isn't going to be a lot of fun."

"Do you think Jackie will go to the police?" I asked.

"I'm sure Gordon's already working on her to keep that from happening. He can be very persuasive. He knows how to use incentives—both positive and negative. By now Harkins must know, too, and I'm sure he'll be working his magic on her as well."

"Shit. I hope he doesn't hurt her."

There was another pause. "Not hurt her? Donnie, how many times has he pimped her out to his buddies? He's never going to *stop* hurting her."

"I mean, he won't kill her or rough her up, will he?"

"Not if she keeps quiet."

"That's a hell of a big if, Vince."

"Donnie." Vince's voice was suddenly hard and cold. "You screwed up. You have to pay. So will Jackie if she doesn't keep her mouth shut. But Gordon and Harkins and all those guys aren't going to get that upset. Shit like this has happened before."

"It has?"

"Uh-huh. They know how to silence people. They're experts at the strategic use of fear." He let that hang in the air. "Listen, I'll do what I can for you. Harkins knows how valuable you are to him. You're good at following orders and getting things done. My guess is he'll tolerate one screw-up. He might fire you, or he might just bust your balls, make you grovel a little, and let you keep your job. It's not like you're selling company secrets."

Now it was my turn to pause. "Okay, man," I said. "Thanks."

"Bye, Donnie."

I went into the kitchen, where Carol was washing her and Jason's breakfast dishes.

"Who called, honey?"

"My boss."

"What did he want?"

"I'll find out at nine."

She looked at me. "Is it good news or bad news?"

"Good. I hope. I'll let you know."

"Donnie, Penney's is having a sale, and Jason needs new sneakers."

I pulled out my wallet, handed her a ten, and gave her a peck on the cheek.

"Thanks, honey."

I stared glumly at the crumbs on the kitchen table. If only the problems at the station could be fixed with a ten spot and a kiss.

32

Tuesday, September 7, 1976
Billboard Hot 100 Hit Song of the Week:
"You Should Be Dancing" by The Bee Gees

I got in at 9:00 and hurried down the hall, passing Jackie's office. She was sitting at her desk, engrossed in a phone call, like nothing had happened.

There weren't any niceties when I got to Gordon's. He was sitting at his desk, reading, and didn't even look up when I walked in.

"Shut the door, Donnie."

I shut the door and took a seat across the desk from him.

For a few seconds, he kept reading. Then he sighed and looked up at me. There was fury in his eyes. He said in a low growl, "You fucked up big-time, you lightweight."

I let out a long breath. "Who told you?" I asked.

"Tony. He's trying to keep his job."

"He was supposed to leave her alone. He promised me he wouldn't touch her. He's the one who messed up. He promised me..." I was wasting my breath.

Slowly, Gordon raised his palm. "Donnie, shut up."

I did.

"This is on you, Donnie. You were in charge. This was your big chance. You should have been watching Tony. She shouldn't have woken up."

"She was supposed to wake up in the morning on the couch," I said. " It was all planned out."

"Well, that didn't happen, and you handled it 100% wrong. You're a moron."

I sat silently in front of Gordon, not knowing what to say.

"You could go to prison for this," he said.

Suddenly I couldn't stop myself. "I'm not the only one who could go to prison over this," I said.

Gordon stood up and placed his clenched fists on the desk. For a moment I thought he was going to come over and strangle me. Then he did something even more frightening—he smiled. And then he sat back down.

"I can keep her quiet," Gordon said matter-of-factly. "I can keep the jocks quiet, too. I'll feed them some bullshit about her taking money on the side. I've seen this before and I know what to do. But the question is, can I keep *you* quiet and obedient? Or do we need to take extreme measures?"

Suddenly Gordon was talking about "we" instead of "I."

"I know how to keep quiet," I said softly.

Gordon nodded. "From now on, you're going to follow orders exactly, Donnie. To the letter. Any deviation, however small, and your career in radio is over. And that might not be the only thing that ends."

I had already been following Elizabeth's orders to the letter. But I knew not to open my mouth. I just nodded.

"Now," Gordon said. "Fire Jackie. Immediately."

"What do I tell her? What reason should I give?

"Just go in her office and fire her. Give her ten minutes to leave the premises. You don't need a reason. Tell her she'll get her last paycheck in the mail. Make sure she doesn't take anything before she goes, especially her Rolodex. I don't want her calling anyone in the business."

"Do you think she'll go quietly?" I asked. "What if she makes a scene, or begs to keep her job?"

Gordon looked at me with an expression of supreme disgust. "Donnie, you're a clueless dipshit. If you have to, come get me and I'll call the cops to have her escorted out. On second thought, I'll just stand by the reception area and watch. If there's a problem, I'll call the police myself. Got that?"

"Yes."

"Now, you need a cover story. Something you can tell the jocks and anyone who asks," said Gordon. "Say she took payola. And if anyone asks more questions, make it clear that if they don't shut up, they'll be the next one out the door."

"Do you think she'll go to the police? What if she gets a lawyer?"

"If she had gone to the police, we would have heard by now. If she lawyers up, we can manage it."

"But what if she—"

"*Donnie!*" Gordon shouted. "Get your sorry ass out of here. *Now.*"

I got up to go. As I reached the door, Gordon said, "You haven't heard the end of this, Donnie."

I left and closed the door behind me—a bit too hard.

Now I had to go face Jackie.

I walked directly into Jackie's little office and shut the door behind me. She was off the phone and writing something on her notepad. After a few seconds, she put down her pen and looked at me.

Her eyes were dilated and watery. She didn't say a word—just sat and stared at me.

I thought of when I first hired her back in Beach City. She had been so bubbly and enthusiastic then.

I looked at her blue eyes and curly hair, her toes sticking out of her platform sandals, her cute bell-bottoms. She was wearing a Midwest Music FM T-shirt.

I just blurted it out. "Jackie, you're fired."

She still didn't say anything to me. She just sat there. No talking, no questions, no pleading, no cajoling, no crying. No reaction at all.

She gave me the tiniest of nods. Then she opened her desk drawer, took out her green tapestry hippie bag, put it over her shoulder, stood up, and walked out. She didn't turn around or look back.

I followed her as she made her way through the office. I watched her open the front door and walk out to the elevator.

I stood there inside the office, looking through the glass door while she waited for the elevator. It arrived, she entered, and then she disappeared.

I turned around. Standing there, watching, were Gordon Taylor, his secretary Elaine, and our receptionist Claudia.

"Okay, everyone," Gordon said angrily. "Show's over. Let's get back to work.

33

Friday, September 10, 1976
Billboard Hot 100 Hit Song of the Week:
"You Should Be Dancing" by The Bee Gees

Jackie was gone, and I was still treading on thin ice around the office. I kept getting phone messages from people who were looking for her. I ignored them all.

Then, on Friday, when I came back from lunch, there was an open newspaper sitting on my desk. I had no clue who had put it there, or why.

I picked up the paper. It was *Rock Concert Times,* one of those throwaway papers they give out free at record stores. Jackie had been interviewed by the paper a week or so before she left. Now here was the interview in black and white, literally under my nose.

The paper was folded to page four, to the article about Jackie. There was a large picture of her sitting cross-legged on a patchwork pillow on the floor. She was holding a set of headphones and wearing jeans and a sweater. A pole light with a swivel neck illuminated the background.

The caption under the picture said, "Jackie Phillips, music director."

Janet Merran

Midwest Music FM—
Where It's a Woman's World for Picking the Hits
by Margie Bettendorf, *Rock Concert Times* staff writer

Midwest Music FM is one of the highest-rated Top 40 stations in our city. The station is geared for general listeners, but it appeals mainly to young adults ages 18 to 24. Jackie Phillips is the station's very first woman music director, and she has a lot of responsibility. In a recent interview, she discussed the scientific research that determines the station's playlist.

THE SOUNDS OF THE CITY

"Our station plays the music popular in our area," Jackie explained. "This is a special place, and our station responds to its listeners. We play many songs that aren't heard in other markets. We have a unique sound that is ours alone."

Every week Jackie calls record stores in the metropolitan area. She builds relationships with the store personnel and compiles their top sales. The station also makes direct callouts, asking the public about their favorite songs and what stations they listen to. "It's not an easy process," Jackie told me. "But it's important to keep on top of the trends.

"But not everyone who listens to Midwest Music FM buys records," she added. "I put the numbers from the sales and call-outs together to get an accurate picture of what our listeners want."

Top 40 stations are known for playing singles, but Jackie is convinced that album and 8-track sales are a more important reflection of an artist's strength. "When a particular artist gets an overwhelming response on the request lines, the station will play album cuts. On Sunday evenings we have the Favorites Countdown, and the request lines go crazy. That's a good time to try out a song from an album." This combined approach to music programming gives the station a wide variety and a great balance of artists.

"Our station has the widest variety of music in the area," Jackie explained. "The sound is for both black and white audiences. What we do is unique."

A CAREER IN RADIO

Jackie grew up on the east coast, constantly listening to the radio. She went to City University, where she got her degree in communications. She worked at her college radio station in her junior and senior years.

Jackie said, "I got started in college and wanted to make it my career. I have family in Beach City and went there after graduation to find a job in radio. At first,

I worked at a college station as an intern. I was even a DJ. Eventually I was hired at Midwest Music FM's sister station. I started by answering the request lines. I was promoted to secretary and assistant to the program director."

PRESSURES OF THE BUSINESS

Jackie admitted that she is sensitive to the pressures of the business. "It really isn't a job you forget about when you leave the office," she confided. "Even at home I listen to our competition, preview new music, and read the trade journals."

"I really love radio," Jackie added. "We all work together as a team. We hang out together and talk shop wherever we go. It's like a secret society. Even though I'm one of the few women in my position, I look up to the national music director of our chain, who is also a woman. We talk on a weekly basis about the new music."

TEAMWORK

"At Midwest Music FM, we realize that radio is more than just a sound that comes over the air," Jackie said, gesturing for emphasis. "You can't put your finger on it. We develop the image of the station with the music, personalities, and contests. It's loads of fun because of the high energy. Every DJ has their own rotation of songs, but they can use their creativity, too. That's what makes our station's sound so compelling."

"Midwest Music FM always puts its listeners first. The station uses research and a special formula, but the people who work at the station are very aware of their audience. The station communicates and entertains in a fast and friendly way."

Jackie reflected on her station's philosophy: "Many times, we've discussed whether the station should direct or reflect what people like. But at the end of the day, people just want to be entertained. In the car, at home, or wherever they listen, people just want to hear the music they really enjoy."

I didn't know whether to laugh, cry or puke.

I slowly folded up the paper. Then, in a fit of anger, I tore it up, crunched it into a ball and threw it in the trash can.

34

Thursday, September 15, 1976
Billboard Hot 100 Hit Song of the Week:
"(Shake, Shake, Shake) Shake your Booty" by K.C. and The Sunshine Band

Things still weren't right at the station. The fallout from firing Jackie hadn't slowed down at all. Too many people had questions I couldn't answer. Some of the DJs gave me the evil eye and Marlene kept hammering me for details. At least twenty industry guys asked me what had happened to her. I tried to ignore them or change the subject. When they pressed me, I said she quit because of family problems. Everyone in radio knows that's code for "shut up and stop asking questions."

It was a big deal to get her to come to Midwest Music. She was the first female music director at the station. Then, all of a sudden and for no apparent reason, she was gone.

Even worse, Gordon Taylor still hadn't talked to me about a contest for the ratings sweep next month. For two weeks, I kept trying to get in to see him, so I could pitch my contest ideas, and Elaine kept telling me he wasn't available. Finally, said she was able to get me in at six-thirty tonight.

Then something else happened. We always got paid on the 15th and on the last day of the month. The DJs got their checks mailed. But for us full-time employees, the station bookkeeper came around and dropped our checks on our desks. When I got to my desk around mid-morning, there wasn't a check waiting for me.

I asked Marlene if she had gotten her paycheck.

"Yeah, I did, Donnie. It was on my desk when I came in. I put it in my purse already."

That was a bad omen.

I called Joanne, our bookkeeper. She said, "Yeah, I cut your check yesterday. But Mr. Taylor told me to give it directly to him.

Shit. The jig was up.

I made a quick plan. I scanned my Rolodex, thinking who might hire me. I got out a pen and a few sheets of paper, wrote down all the contacts I thought I would need, folded up the pages, and stuffed them in my pocket.

I looked around the office, trying to memorize every detail. I was all but certain that this would be my last day at Midwest Music FM.

At six-thirty, I started walking slowly to Gordon Taylor's office.

The office staff had already left for the day. The place was empty.

Steve Sullivan was on the air, and I could hear his patter over the opening chords of Wild Cherry's "Play That Funky Music."

"Midwest... Music... FM! Bringing you the hottest hits on the coolest nights! Are you ready for some funky music? Get down, get down! Here's some Wild Cherry. I'm Steve Sullivan on Midwest... Music... FM!"

Gordon's door was closed, so I knocked.

"Come in, Donnie."

I opened the door and entered.

Gordon Taylor and Henry Harkins were waiting for me, both seated, and both glaring straight at me.

"Sit down, Donnie," Gordon said, softly but firmly. "We have some things to talk about."

This was it. I sat.

Henry Harkins pointed at me. "You're leaving this station and the Harkins chain, effective immediately. When you leave this room, you'll have five minutes to clean out your office and go. If you don't, we'll call the police and have you arrested for trespassing. Got that?"

I nodded. "Got it."

Harkins frowned deeply. "You embarrassed the station, Donnie, and you embarrassed Harkins Media. I can't have a guy like you working for a company with my name on it."

The next thing I knew, I was standing up again. "A guy like me? *I'm* the corrupt one? Screw you, Henry. I'm a radio programmer, not a pimp."

"And you failed at both," said Harkins mildly. "Now sit back down. *Now.*"

Again, I sat.

"We had to pay off the little bitch," Gordon said. "And it wasn't cheap. She had a big-shot lawyer shake us down. So, Mr. Failed Pimp, you won't see any more paychecks from Midwest Music. Including the one you expected today.

"What the hell—," I began.

Harkins held up a hand and pushed his palm forward. The gesture was meant to silence me, but it looked more like a Nazi salute.

"Here's how I look at it, Donnie," he said. "You're lucky we're letting you out of here alive." He stopped and looked thoughtful for a moment, then turned to Gordon. "Did we decide to let this shithead live? Or is that issue still up in the air? What do *you* think we should do to him, Gordon?"

Gordon looked equally thoughtful. "He has a family, doesn't he?"

"We don't want to leave his little wife a widow, do we?"

"Of course not, Henry."

I almost shit myself.

"Should we blackball him from radio?" Harkins asked.

"As much as we can. But he's got too many contacts; we can't control all of them."

"True. He's finished with the big leagues, though. He'll only be able to work in Outer Podunk, Alaska."

"Are you sure that's sufficient punishment?" Gordon asked.

"Maybe not."

"We could throw him in the river."

"Someone might find him."

"Nah, he'd be fish food."

Half of me was terrified, but half of me knew they were just toying with me one final time before kicking me to the curb.

Suddenly I heard my own voice speaking. My brain knew the wisest course was to shut up and sit still, but I couldn't stop myself. "I don't deserve this, Mr. Harkins. I've always been loyal. You know I have."

Harkins and Gordon suddenly went silent. For a few seconds they both stared at me impassively, like two scientists studying an insect.

Then Harkins said softly, "Art Fields."

The bottom dropped out of my stomach.

"Art Fields?" I asked. "The owner of Rivertown Radio? What does he have to do with any of this?"

Harkins shook his head sadly.

"Screw you, Donnie," Gordon said. "Art sent me a copy of the ratings book you sold him. Art double-crossed you, Donnie. He played you."

Harkins gave me another tight, evil smile. "An Organization media company just bought Rivertown Radio," he said. "They're making a public announcement tomorrow. And then they're changing the format. Art Fields is a millionaire now. Too bad for you, Donnie."

That's when I lost it. I was back on my feet, shouting. "You're a sick man, Henry—a sick, sick man. You *enjoy* what you do to those girls. And you ruined Jackie. She was a nice girl, and all she wanted was a decent job. Why did you have to use her? One day she's going to tell everyone. She'll write a goddamn book about you and your criminal, psychopathic pals."

I was on a roll, and I couldn't stop. "And you want to talk about Art Fields? You know what he told me? He knew all about what you did to Jackie. He said he couldn't believe you would stoop so low. And you know what else? He said if Jackie was his daughter, he'd shoot you dead."

I waited for more to erupt out of me, but nothing more came. I sat down.

The room was quiet for a few seconds as we all caught our breath. Then both men stood up.

Harkins looked at me coldly. "You've got five minutes. Gather your things and leave. Don't take anything that isn't yours. That includes the Rolodex. Gordon will accompany you to your office to make sure you only take your personal items. Your career in major-market radio is over." He paused and took a deep breath. "Goodbye, Donnie."

I stood up and looked at Henry Harkins for the last time. "Goodbye, Henry. And screw you."

Gordon walked me to my office. He stood by the door as I gathered up my family photos and a few personal items. I stuffed everything in a little box I had on a shelf. It took me less than two minutes.

"I've got it all," I said. "I'm ready."

"Okay, let's go."

We walked together to the front door. Gordon silently held it open for me.

I looked at him one last time, expecting to see fury or disgust in his eyes. But he wasn't even looking at me. He was scanning the scheduling board across the room.

I ducked out without looking back.

Back on the street again, I found my way to my Camaro. I threw my crap on the seat, got behind the wheel, and grabbed a joint I had hidden in the glove box. I lit it up and started the car for the drive back home. For the first time in my entire life, I didn't turn on the car radio.

That was it—the end of my time as a program director for the best Top 40 chain in the country.

I drove around for a while to finish the doob and then drove through a Steak 'n Shake for some coffee. Then I sat in my car in the parking lot, thinking about how to tell Carol that we'd have to move—again. Carol was just starting to make friends, and now it was time to pack up all over again.

Now I was just like Jackie. Out in the cold. And, just like her, I had gotten played. I'd always known it was going to end. I just never guessed it would end so soon.

I sighed and turned the key in the ignition. Now I had to go home and face the music.

At eight-thirty, I got home and quietly let myself in. Jason was in bed and Carol was watching TV. She waved to me and blew me a kiss. I blew one back.

There was no way I could tell Carol tonight that we needed to tear Jason away from his new school, and that the life we were trying to create here was over. I needed to be alone.

Also, I wanted to snort a bump and talk to Vince.

I went into the bedroom and locked the door. As soon as I was buzzed, I lit a cig and dialed his home number.

Vince answered on the second ring. "Hello."

"Vince, it's me, Donnie."

"Yeah, I've been expecting your call," he said sadly.

"I screwed everything up, Vince."

"Yeah, you did." There was some empathy in his voice, but there was a hardness behind it. "Donnie, what the hell were you thinking? Selling Bailey's research? That was really stupid, man."

"I couldn't stand to watch them hurt those girls," I said.

"You were in on it, Donnie, every step of the way. You could have bailed at the first sign of trouble. Other guys have."

He had a point.

Vince said, "How do you think you got the job at Beach City Radio in the first place? The previous program director got wind of some of the shit Harkins is into and got out."

"You're right, Vince. It would have been better if I had bailed early on."

"Hindsight is 20/20, buddy."

"None of this is why I went into radio."

"Yeah, I know, it sucks. None of it was why any of us got into radio. Except maybe Harkins. There are a lot of things we do in this business that we don't like. But it is what it is."

"Do you think you can pull some strings for me?" I asked. "Help me find a new job in a smaller market?"

"You've got a good résumé," Vince said. "You'll land on your feet."

"But can you help me?""

"No." He paused for a few seconds.

"Okay, I get it."

"It was a hell of a ride, Donnie, but we both knew it would end sometime."

"Yeah."

"Oh, and Donnie...Don't call me again. I can't help you anymore."

35

Saturday, January 1, 2000
Billboard Hot 100 Hit Song of the Week:
"Smooth" by Santana

Somehow, we all got away with it. Nobody went to jail; nobody even got arrested. As far as I know, nobody even got investigated.

Now, almost 25 years later, some of us are still in radio; most of us got out. Some are gone and some are in their twilight years, but none of us ever got caught. The men all pretended like it never happened, and the girls were all too scared to say anything.

Nowadays we could never get away with the things we did back then. People are smarter, and there are cameras everywhere. I guess that's a good thing.

There have been so many changes in the radio biz that I hardly recognize it anymore. The days of the boss jock are long gone, replaced by a guy in a studio recording digital programs. There are almost no family-owned stations, except in the smallest markets. The government changed everything when they allowed consolidation and multiple-station ownership in the same market.

Top 40 isn't even that popular, not the way it used to be. Hip-hop has taken over, and so has country music. I don't even recognize the songs anymore.

Harkins Media stations were sold in the late 1980s to one of the big conglomerates, and Harkins put his money into international investment funds. He died ten years ago, and as far as I know, none of his heirs followed him into the Organization. They're all clean-cut types with regular jobs.

Earl Fredrickson is an old man now. He lives with his wife in one of those senior developments where he plays golf all day. Patrick Thomas saw him at the Beach City station reunion in 1995 and said he has pretty bad memory loss.

Nick Mitchell and Vince Johnson both continued working at Harkins Media for a long time. When it got sold, they started a music consulting business. Their company made music mixes that are played at casinos, resorts, and restaurants. Vince, now in his sixties, is retired in Costa Rica. Nick Mitchell died about six years ago.

After many years, Vince and I patched things up. Just before the Beach City Top 40 reunion in 1995, Vince called me up unexpectedly to ask if I'd been invited. It was great to hear from him, and we spent a lot of time talking about our families and all the different jobs we had over the years.

When he asked me about the reunion, I told him that Patrick had invited me, although it wasn't through official channels. Vince and I agreed that neither one of us would go.

We talked a lot about that stuff we did to chicks back in the day. He was proud of the fact that he never got busted. He admitted that he kept going to bars and messing with chicks until his mid-forties. He'd spike their drinks with the pills and take them to a hotel room to have his fun.

Vince told me about one of the broads—a real looker—who was an executive at a competing radio chain. He said that after he messed with her, she didn't report it to the police. But whenever he saw her again at radio functions, he noticed that she never drank a sip or ate a morsel.

We talked about Elizabeth Corley, too. Elizabeth got out of radio in the early 1980s and opened a public relations firm. Today she has a successful company with a lot of employees. I made a point not to stay in touch with her. The last I heard, she was writing a tell-all about some of her famous PR clients.

Since then, Vince and I call each other occasionally to talk and reminisce. Every year I send him a Christmas card from Carol and me, and he sends us one with palm trees.

Last week I called Vince to catch up, and I finally worked up the nerve to ask him the questions that had nagged at me for decades.

"Listen, Vince. I've got to know. Why Jackie? Why did Harkins focus on her? What was so special about her?"

"I dunno, Donnie. Your guess is as good as mine."

"And in that hotel room—what were those foreign men looking at?"

"You were there, dude. I wasn't."

"They were looking for some kind of mark or cut inside her pussy. What was it? Who did it? Was it the Organization?"

"Maybe. Or maybe a more powerful organization."

"A secret society?"

"That's above my pay grade," Vince said.

"I never talked to Elizabeth again. But you did. Did Elizabeth ever say anything about Jackie, or about those rituals?"

For a few seconds, Vince was silent. Then he said, "Do you really want to know?"

"Hell, yes."

"Okay, then. Elizabeth said Jackie was marked from the beginning."

"Marked? What does that even mean?"

"I don't know. But that's what she said. It was a long time ago."

"What else did she say?" I asked.

"She said she felt sorry for Jackie. So, she didn't do the rituals right—on purpose."

"Huh?"

"That black magic stuff—she said there's a right way and a wrong way to do it. And if you do it the wrong way, it doesn't work."

"Wait," I said. "So, all that black magic shit was real, and not just for show?"

"I have no idea, dude. I'm just telling you what Elizabeth told me. She said that she knew how to do everything properly, but that she deliberately did part of the ritual the wrong way, so Jackie would be protected from the dark forces."

"What dark forces? You mean like the Devil?

Vince snorted. "You tell me, man. I don't know."

"What about when Ray did the same kind of black magic stuff? Was he doing it right or wrong?"

"You'd have to ask him, Donnie. I never even met the guy"

For a few seconds we were both silent.

"Vince," I said, "Those knockout drugs they gave her—do you know anything about them?"

"You remember where we got those drugs, don't you?"

"Yeah, from Nick Mitchell."

"Yeah, but he got them from a top-secret government lab. They were powerful. They were mostly used on captured spies, and in the military."

"How the hell did Nick Mitchell get them?"

"He had friends in high places."

"In the government? In the military?"

"Hell, if I know, man."

"There's one last thing, Vince. The messages."

"What messages?"

"You know—the coded messages we used to broadcast."

"I never did that. That's news to me."

"Are you telling me the truth, Vince?"

"I was in the New York office; nobody told me about any messages."

I sighed. "It was great talking to you, Vince."

"Same here, man."

That was the end of our conversation.

As for the rest of the guys, they've all gone their separate ways. Ben Bailey and Lou Arnold ran their radio consulting business for many years and made a lot of money. Ben is retired now and spends his time with his grandkids and doing charity work. Lou buys and sells vintage sports cars.

Gordon Taylor left the Harkins chain a couple years after me. He moved to Arizona and ran another radio chain with ties to the Organization for almost 20 years until he retired. A few weeks after his retirement he died from a heart attack. His widow and family made out well, and I heard his son is the CEO of some big company in Phoenix.

The DJs are a mixed bag. Some of them stayed in radio and some of them moved on to other careers. Matt West recently died of cancer. I think almost everybody else is still alive, although I only keep in touch with Patrick Thomas.

Rockin' Rex stayed in radio. Now he does an oldies show in LA and runs a website about the good old days of Beach City Top 40. He and Stephanie had a daughter who became a high school teacher.

James Ryan left radio, went to divinity school, and became an assistant pastor at one of those mega-churches. That's about the last thing I'd ever think one of my DJs would do. I guess being a DJ trained him for public speaking and delivering sermons.

Charlie Greene is retired and lives in Mexico, and Sammy Talarico owns a wholesale flower shop near Palm Springs that specializes in orchids. Keith Adams became an architect and got hired by a big firm in Los Angeles.

The Midwest Music FM guys are all over the place. I only hear what's going on with them every once in a while.

That leaves Patrick, Kenny, and Jackie. Patrick is still in radio in the Southwest, spinning oldies. He's had lots of radio jobs through the years, including a gig as a program director in the early 1980s. He always loved radio and will do it until he retires, which should be pretty soon. He was married for a while, and from his pictures I can see he's still handsome. He calls himself "The Silver Fox." He has a steady lady who he's been involved with for years. Me and Carol even visited him two years ago. He's not sad that he was never a radio superstar; he's just happy to be doing what he loves.

Kenny bounced around from station to station, harassing female co-workers until one got a lawyer and filed a complaint with the state. But they couldn't make it stick—at the last minute, a key witness chickened out. He's out of the radio business now. He works in a casino in Laughlin and lives in a trailer with Christine. His wife ate herself into type 2 diabetes, and that was after a round of breast cancer.

And then there's Jackie.

I never really got over her. I still have pictures of her that I keep in a locked box in the attic. Every once in a while, when Carol isn't home, I take them out and look at them.

Ironically, Jackie is doing the best of all of us. After what happened, she should have ended up in the loony bin or dead of an overdose. But she's wealthy, successful, and, from the pictures I've seen, still beautiful.

After I fired her from Midwest Music, she picked up and moved back east to work for Red Kleinman at his radio trade journal. After a couple of years, she went back to graduate school and got herself an M.B.A. and a lawyer husband. Today they're both corporate professionals.

She has two kids in high school and lives in one of those fancy McMansions. Besides her job, she does charity work. I wonder if she still goes to Todd Rundgren concerts. I heard he still tours.

I don't know if her memory ever came back. I've been afraid for years that she would figure things out and show up at my door with a gun. And that charity she volunteers for—it helps women who are survivors of domestic violence and sexual abuse.

Carol and I are doing all right. I'm sure the only reason she didn't divorce me after the fiasco at Midwest Music FM was because she was pregnant. I got a DJ job in Memphis and Heather was born in 1977. That Memphis job turned out to be a godsend. Nothing about it was shady, except a little payola here and there. It saved our marriage, and with my stress levels reduced, I got my health back.

The job lasted a couple years, and I would have stayed there forever, but a new owner changed the format, so it was time to move on again. I kept looking for gigs as a program director, but it was impossible. Harkins and the Organization successfully blackballed me. I could only get DJ and music director jobs in smaller markets.

Heather and Jason grew up like Army brats, moving every few years from one town to the next, while I took one crappy radio job after another. I worked in Florida, Texas, Wyoming, and Arizona. Eventually we ended up in Ohio.

Carol went back to work as soon as Heather started school. First, she was a nurse's aide, which was a good job for us since she could get hired quickly whenever we moved. Then, when we were more settled, Carol got a job as an administrative assistant at an insurance company. That helped ease the financial burden of raising two kids.

Jason always resented me, so when he hit high school, we sent him back to Texas to live with his father. That worked out fine, and Jason graduated and went to the University of Texas. He's in Austin now, working in IT. He has a cute girlfriend, and I think he'll pop the question soon. Carol goes by herself to visit him a couple of times a year.

Jason's leaving eased things up a lot for us, and we were able to take a lot better care of Heather. She grew into a gorgeous girl with long, thick dark hair like her mom's. After much debate, she got breast implants for her eighteenth birthday. When I was young, I always liked girls with the natural look, but that's what she wanted.

Heather was always interested in acting, so after a couple of years at college, she moved to LA She makes a passable living doing bit roles in television and commercials.

Sometimes we send money to Heather between her acting jobs. I really miss her, and we're planning a trip to LA this summer to visit her and a couple of my old radio friends.

Now we're empty nesters with both kids pretty far away, which leaves us time for travel and hobbies.

I got out of radio for good in 1990. Since Carol was working in insurance, I decided to become an insurance agent and open a small office in our town. Carol and I work together now, and our business has expanded up to the point where I think we can retire when I turn 65.

Sometimes I get out my old tapes and listen to the airchecks. It cracks me up to hear those commercials I produced for jeans stores, car dealerships, and fast-food joints. And I love hearing the promos for those crazy contests.

Last year a book came out about Top 40 radio in Southern California. The author must have had a major obsession with it because he researched and wrote a 150-page history that included every Top 40 station in the area. Our station was prominent in the book.

I heard about the book from Patrick. For some reason, the author never contacted me to ask about my days as program director of Beach City Top 40.

I finally bought a copy. There were two pages of blurbs about each of the jocks during my years at the station. The author didn't mention Jackie's name, but he used some of her *Hit Sheet* pictures. He mentioned me exactly once and spelled my name wrong. Today I'm just a footnote in the history of Beach City Top 40.

36

Thursday, November 23, 2000
Billboard Hot 100 Hit Song of the Week:
"Independent Women Part 1" by Destiny's Child

D onnie, did you hear that voice message from Heather?"
I was sitting on the sofa in the den, thinking about old times and watching the Thanksgiving game with the sound on mute. It was the Dallas Cowboys versus the Minnesota Vikings. Carol had just walked in.

"No, honey," I said.

"She must have left the message last night when we were at Applebee's. I didn't see the blinking light until just now. She has exciting news. You should listen to it yourself."

The answering machine was hooked up to the phone in the kitchen. I pressed the play button and sat down at the kitchen table.

Heather's voice was chirping with excitement. "Hi, Mom and Dad! I've got some great news. My agent hooked me up with a big Hollywood star who says he wants to be my mentor. He saw my press kit and called a few days ago."

My stomach clenched.

"Dad, he's really famous—he's a household name. He started in comedy and had a hit TV sitcom. I can't believe it;

he's really interested in my career and said he can do a lot for me. I'm going to meet him at the West Park Hotel in Beverly Hills tonight for drinks. I'll call you tomorrow morning. Love you. Bye."

I turned off the message without deleting it.

Carol came back into the room. "I wonder who she was meeting?"

Before I knew what I was saying, I blurted out, "Do you think she's okay?"

Carol looked at me.

I said, "I'm concerned. You know, it's easy for a young woman to be taken advantage of these days."

Carol looked at me some more, with an expression I'd never seen before. She said, "Heather told us she'd call this morning. It's almost 8:00 p.m."

I looked down at my hand. It was trembling.

"I'm sure we'll hear from her in a little bit," I said. "She's a not naïve, and that actor's got a reputation to uphold." Even to me the words sounded unconvincing.

"You're worried, too," Carol said softly.

We were both quiet for a few seconds. Carol went to the counter and began heating up water in the tea kettle.

Then she turned and looked at me. "Donnie," she said. "I knew everything that was going on at those radio stations."

I looked at her. I knew better than to say a word.

"I knew about the blowjobs. I knew about the cocaine. And I knew about the payola."

I nodded slowly. "All true," I said softly, flooded with relief that those were the only things she was aware of. She kept looking at me, her face impassive. I could see that she expected a better response.

"Carol, I'm sorry. That was a long time ago, and things were different."

"You're lucky I didn't divorce you back then."

"I'm lucky, too."

She sighed. "I'm worried about our daughter."

"I am, too. But I'm also excited for her. Maybe this will be her big break."

The knot in my stomach tightened.

THE END

About the Author

Janet Merran received her Master's degree from the University of Minnesota, and attended classes at the Loft Literary Center. As an insider in Top 40 radio in the 1970's, she experienced its culture and many of its seamier practices firsthand. *Top 40 Honeypot* is fictional, but it is based on a real era, industry, and culture. This is her first novel.